The  from the checkout counter into the cereal aisle. I sought purchase of two packages: a four-pound bundle of rainbow trout and one bag of freshly fried chicken (cooked on the premises). I'd watched the seafood attendant splay, clean and fillet the fish, lobbied for wings at the lunch counter, and now stood at the line's end. Behind shining lenses of Ray-Ban sunglasses, scars from my abortive apprenticeship and concealed deceit parade and flitter. An elderly gentleman at the head of the line fumbles anxiously for his wallet. His face reflects a sense of questioning. Fact is, his entire body is shaped like a huge question mark: head bent forward, shoulders curled, chest slumped forward, arms splayed from his sides. We know him! screams my eyes and remain riveted to this cobra-like line's head. The rhythms of those effortless meat attendant's strokes to splay and fillet the trout swim inside my sunglasses. The strokes slice into rhythm templates as I watch this question-mark and as if by magic, more question-marks ensue—a division, yet multiplied.

    Personal memory tumbles backwards, freighted with a question-mark as its locomotive. Distracted by the scent of fish, fried wings and breasts of chicken, I can't quite put a name to the face. An explosion of memory yanks me to clarity and I say to myself: Hargrove! He steams forward a single green flag, huffs an appreciative glance at the attendant, demands a receipt, and nods graciously. Behind my glasses, my scars blossom crimson, then fade. Faces I had known a halo. Yes!

Wesley Hargrove—gatekeeper of the Golden West, esteemed critic of the local paper, cultural czar of the Memphis arts community, chastity-belt of artistic enterprise.

The dimmed sight reminds me of my own journey towards mastery, of the personalities I'd met along the way, of this little old man steeped in the finance and attitudes of a by-gone era. As disengaged onlooker, I study him as he pays his bill, shuffles his cart to the door, and melts out of sight. It has been a decade since I'd seen him last. Later, on my way home, his lingering image prompted me to stop at old French Fort, recline against my sacred magnolia tree, take a ruffled quill from my glove compartment, and recollect this tale, even as fried chicken wings steamed the interior of my car. I began unloading the freight of memory, spilled it onto paper, tracked and trailed it like a red caboose. Old Wesley Hargrove had indeed played his part in my journey.

I think back over that first encounter with M3, rummage through my memories and diverse impressions. Like clouds in the sky, these impressions glide, morph, and reform leaving images—some clear, others muddy. Would I reject the whole, embrace nothing from that era in my life? No! thunders my heart to hoist my brain, no! Those days form the bricks of what I have become, those days of newness and mastery revealed and paths unclear—those days marked in refrains and revelations.

I came to my Master, some say maestro, from the street though I was not a block boy. He came to me, not for a slave, but in search of an apprentice; his plucked grape was his vision. In truth, we were both learners in the manufacture of fresh wisdom, both pilgrims carving paths untrodden, from nihilism to sculpture art. For now, let's call him master, though untutored in the braided hum of whip and certainly no magician of baton. I reeked of ignorance in artful design, unfettered to discipline in drawing, and uncoupled to passion or vision as my carrot.

I use the term *Master* with deep reservation, as the term hoots with much historical (mostly negative) baggage in southern climes, especially for those of us ensconced like pearls in oysters of negritude. Let us temporarily banish *Master* and deploy maestro for mastery, since that term bugles the chase and brings the story closer to view. As one of ancestry mixed, multiplied by parentage known and unknown, imagination shudders even with parchment-shimmed efforts to emboss the lineage I now represent. Cherokee, Nordic, African, Scot? Past one century, it would be difficult, if not impossible, to assign dominance to which bloodline carouses in my veins. Is a DNA analysis in my future? Perhaps boisterous basslines, thundering and assaulting metropolitan traffic can ferret that out in rap! Mastery, Maestro, Master, slave or apprentice, learner or block boy?

Suffice it to say that my Master soon-to-be Maestro of sculpture and design and painting exhibited an imagination *par excellence*. Breathtaking drawings, designs, and sketches cantered from his pen. As tenderloin and burgher, one of scant years and the other of scant career, we had stumbled upon one another on Main Street by fortuitous accident. His stumble was my gain! I labored to chalk and spray graffiti sketches on concrete slabs in front of his studio, directly beneath Amtrak's north/south railroad tracks. Blight choked the area and my crude artistry brought color to gray brick. Formerly condemned to the wrecking ball, his studio had been spared, declared livable, and revived to its new existence by his obdurate determinism. Where before the studio slumped in slovenly disgrace, it now sported long metal portals skirted with sandblasted mortar and panes of elongated glass. Its front, gated with an iron door, stood forth with the bricked elegance of a lawyer's office. Upon seeing my pathetic scribbles, he'd jibed, Hey boy—bring some of that energy over here!

    Though energetic, I had yet to experience passionate release and was thought to be thin of physique and pliable of mind. In dress I was simple yet clean and of life plan short-sighted and reckless, perhaps inclined to academic truancy. At the time, I'd been on the prowl for errands and employment of a part-time variety. In short, I could be happy with anything that brought extra coin my way. In hindsight, I wonder now if *soon-to-be* saw merit in my little chalk sketch. Even so, I experience a jolt of inner fracture, a tension that punts logic and jabs the heart—Mastro or Maester—but this journey would take me closer to understanding differences between apprentice and slave, learner and truant (to craft and vision). Imagine my joy upon entering this studio, this house of imagery: amulets, bright paintings, half-fashioned sculptures of clay, photos of every size and shape, and mounds of dust—both airborne and underfoot—charmed its spaces.

Okay! I answered, passing my gaze beyond the haze of dust and lighting upon items both unique and enchanting on studio entry. A large church bell, embellished with a track for pulleys and silver-golden in color stood closest to me. Its hue (a word I learned much later) owned a mirror-like tinge and its track suggested ropes to be operated by hand. It stood on braces and possessed miniature faces of Malcom X and Martin King. Below it stood a For Sale sign. From time to time the Maestro (he hated the word Master as he relegated it to the antebellum period) would ring the bell where it stood, comically saying, Finally a church bell rings in Memphis for Martin, and chuckle to himself.

Later I would find this Maestro was in word and deed a gentleman, so I addressed him as neither Master nor Maestro, but by name. My own designation was murky in my mind; was I apprentice or a slave? As you might imagine, he was a proud person of color, with a small dose of harnessed conceit to fashion his stage. A long trail of walled diplomas in tongues foreign to my decipher ran smack into my gaze. Noticing my appraisal he said, I am in need of a helper, an apprentice, who can help me around my shop, perform minor labor, run small errands, and be generally useful. I see you have an artistic eye and a flare for form. Do you have an appetite for such a job?

In my prison of naiveté, I knew practically nothing of apprenticeship, thinking that the job would be simple and I would spend time in the presence of these mysterious artifacts. You pay by the hour? I asked, lost in the bizarre appearances of objects, sliced into layers of function (later I learned in the style of Damien Hirst) and small paintings rendered naturally and teeming with color. Though financial impoverishment vented his days, a fertility of imagination revealed his penchant for the engineer's question: How does this work?

One of the most telling phrases he uttered after ringing that church bell (he called it M3) was, It bongs and swings as if it were a living, breathing thing. Indeed, it was a strange affair, sitting there in a studio filled with odd statues, items in various stages of sculpture, a dusty old chessboard dotted with one or two broken pieces and plumed with a jester's cap, a large pine box (he said it reminded him of his mortality) with lid closed, mottled on its side by one knotty hole, a broad panoramic photo of featherbells, and an ungodly assortment of hammers, chisels, brushes, paints, sketches and drawings. This mess was covered in the same thin layer of dust that had carpeted the chessboard. I asked, How much will you pay me? as he conducted ellipses, parabolas, angled lines, circles, and elaborate contusions and combinations of these shapes on paper, drawing as we chatted. *I've seen those same movements in basketball games.* It was as if he were a cartoonish conductor of some invisible orchestra, only his movements were effected in change of color, dimension, and shape on paper instead of in sound.

My name is Afri, he said, I'll pay you seven bucks an hour and a bonus of one dollar for every feather you gather and turn into a quill. As time passed, I listened to his stories of sculptor Henry Kirke Brown's apprentice by the name of John Quincy Adams Ward. Ward had spent seven years as Brown's apprentice and was responsible for a statue called the Freedman. The photo occupied a prominent place in this Main Street studio of Maestro Afri and displayed much less dust than the other items. These anatomies, statues, bells and even photos were tinged with an energy that conspired to jolt them into motion. As requested, I gave my attention to gathering feathers of many shapes and sizes to adapt and turn into quills. In fact, I use a quill made of a hawk's feather to scribe this very tale.

My main job was to dust. On occasion, I was thrust into the position of cook as my Master—I mean my Maestro—would embark on the journey of his day quite early, determined to capture whatever fleeting images had captured the eye of his mind. With the fervor of a madman, he would peel away layers of skin, then muscle and sinew, revealing a chosen layer of bone or tissue, stark in revelation, chilling to the naked eye. From time to time he would invoke these images—he called them his butterflies—on paper. I often traced and copied those models; my copies lacked depth, were frozen, ill-shaped and waxed devoid of perspective and accuracy. The most interesting characteristic of Maestro Afri's creations was a tendency—a tingling towards aliveness; my gaze expected motion at any given moment. It was a trait he shared with Ward's The Freedman—a naturalism that verged on the very edge of movement, quickness, and vivacity. By contrast, I then possessed no grip on the magic that elevates cheek or chin to even terrestrial, much less into mythic beauty.

    This African-American mentor stalked the vector of two pillars of African-American psyche, attempting to free the black personae of the three-hundred plus years of bondage that yet gripped its spirit at the dawn of the 21st century. I had not fully understood his zealotry then, his seeking of unique and personal pathway between the long, titanic shadows of militant Malcom X and non-violent Martin King; I had not fully digested the efforts of Ida Wells and W.E.B. DuBois, and certainly did not appreciate fully the humanism of Douglass or Senghor. Seven dollars an hour? Sounds good to me! I said. Martin and Malcom, though flip sides in philosophy, had both been silenced by the gun. Could this wizard of movement transform himself to achieve the artistry necessary to sculpt pieces exposing racism's anachronisms? Would he too find himself silenced by guns in the midst of the 21st century?

These scribes of my quill tremble in recording this memoir of my days—the sights and sounds of eye and ear, the folktale that bore revelation. Mine is the attempt to capture the arc and angle, to probe and untangle his motions. He carved his psyche in matter, ordered time and space in trajectories, orbits, loops, ellipses and measurements. Those movements rest invisible to the naked eye and seem performed in vacuous space, etched in frost as if on a winter's window. What did I learn? *My* inky magic this quill incites and carves hieroglyphs on the spaces of this page—but I tarry, let me begin the telling of my story.

II

A spring walk on a Memphis day can ricochet between thunderous darkness and transcendent sunshine, just like Memphis politics. The metallic smell preceding a real scorcher forklifts the sun upwards and turns roads to griddles. Schlitz, a member of our gang, was usually at my door at dawn, ready to make the trek to school. We called him Parrot; the gang was called Las Siestas (which translates into The Naps—of which we had aplenty).

Schlitz had a huge Afro, and a meek way of knocking on the door—I always grinned thinking of it as a nappy rap—which started out really softly and then became louder and slower. I lived with my grandma, which I won't get into because of embarrassment. Now, the way Schlitz got his name is kinda funny and I remember it because he and I are about the same color, with him leaning more towards the red and me leaning more towards the orange. Maybe that is why the sun chased me in particular, trying to leach into the orange in me. It wasn't quite barbecue hot yet, but you could tell that the temperature would be stuck on hot before long. The story goes that Parrot was named Schlitz by his parents, who thought him the same color of brown as the emblem on a Schlitz beer can. His mom loved that kind of beer and might even have had one the night before he was born; it would account for a lot! Anyway, like I said, we called him Parrot because of a mighty stutter.

Sometimes, if it rained late in the day, a cloudy mist would rise from the road, which would sizzle like a griddle frying bacon and smolder with steam. But that would happen early. We had a school travel routine. Usually Parrot and I would next collect Bay Brother by just crossing the street and walking two doors down. We would get to Bay Brother's crib just before passing Mrs. Carmichael's house. Mrs. Carmichael had a stand of bamboo plants that stood at least six-feet tall and sported leaves real thick and healthy. That army of bamboo plants was a standing source of hollowed out bamboo guns; you could get five or six guns out of one stalk. Each of us had one of those guns housed in our pocket, backpack, or waistband. Mrs. Carmichael used to come sashaying out of her house yacking and waving a rolling pin or broom. I done told you boys to stop chopping at my bamboo stand! she said. She lived close to those water canals that flow through Memphis as rainwater drainage ditches.

By the time we got to LeMarcus' house, the sun cast long morning shadows away from our feet. We hipped and hopped on the way to school teasing those shadows like pistons on one of those old steam locomotives that you see on Soul Train. LeMarcus was the only one of us who had a dad in the house. His dad was ex-military and Muslim. The Persian machete he had on the wall still drips blood on my memory. One time I saw his dad on his knees, bowed to the east, and chanting. I knew nothing of Islam morning prayer but was both captivated and impressed; jihad was foreign to my vocabulary.

Most of us had only a book or two, but LeMarcus' dad made him carry a backpack to and from school; he maintained that just from carrying around books, osmosis dictated that learning would take place. Most of my buddies didn't read so hot, 'cept for me and LeMarcus. Before my mom died she bought me a computer and put a Bud Foote reading tutor on it saying, Boy, I ain't worked this hard to raise a dummy—you better believe you gone read real good and bring home good grades. Both me and LeMarcus read above grade level—which wasn't so important to me then—these days I have much more respect for the skill.

Domino and Zorro joined us two blocks from school; Domino's motto was, All for one and one for all! Once Zorro spotted Parrot, he would order him to repeat Domino's motto; intimidated, Parrot would stammer and stutter, causing hoots and howls for a block and a half (Bay Brother would shadow box in the air, mimicking the clack of Parrot's words). Say what? teased Zorro; Zorro loved to tease and draw comic book characters. Occasionally I would notice a feather, but wouldn't go out of my way to make one my property. That changed when Zorro targeted, aimed, blew, and snuffed a Blue Jay with his blowgun. The crimson crest of blood on its breast bore the identical shape of that Persian machete. Yo y'all! said Zorro; he got a big kick from that moment.

LeMarcus would add, Semper Fi! and Parrot would mimic, S-S-semper F-Fi!

By now, the whole world knew that we were almost at the school's pearly gates, with us skylarking, singing, laughing and swapping lies—mainly about each other. Sometimes the school hadn't opened up yet so if that were the case, we would set up the checkerboard that Domino always carried in his backpack and play two or three games of checkers. Sometimes I carried one too, since Granny made me tote my backpack if she had risen when I left for school. Believe you me, we could really get revved up for those checker games. Behind the obvious skill of strategic comprehension—seeing moves abstractly, four or five moves before they would appear, the sunlit checkerboard gave us an opportunity to peer into the psychological posture of each gang member when stressed. Those games were elementary psychology sessions. LeMarcus occasionally became violent and banged or smacked the checkerboard when his position became untenable and loss stared him in the face. Zorro had a similar reaction, especially when his chatter failed and he couldn't verbally confound, tease, or outright cheat an opponent. My knees would quiver and my mind run errands when my mistaken move was exposed. Bay Brother could totally loose concentration; that would severely limit his competitive edge. Domino had an uncanny talent to talk checker strategy—actually talk extensively about *possible* moves–dozens of them, out loud as the game progressed. The opponent's mind would flounce around in refractory mode bamboozled, afraid to comprehend anything, dizzy and afraid to *touch* a checker, for fear of getting laughed at. The whole business of trying to psych the opposition, by mumbling, trash-talking, or verbalizing the dozens could be a very dangerous one. That's for yo nasty momma, or Take this butt-whuppin' home and pin it on yo daddy! said by anyone to another could start fists flying.

Once the checkerboard was cued up, game losses were often followed with the usual excuses and embarrassment. In reflection, I think of those moments as a kind of stretch-lab, a time of seasoning and broadening of personality and keening of observation: who could withstand withering pressure without cracking, who could keep his head and bounce back creatively, who could NOT lose sight of the game and pursue checkerboard victory, who would crack and start to sniffle or shed a tear. Strategic ninjas can be hard to find and are developed under pressure, like diamonds. If the truth be told, clothes could be prime targets for prodigious commentary with the bait set up something like this— Hey bro, that's a mighty sharp shirt you be wearing (and shit)—where'd you find that? Salvation Army? I'm sure most of us have had that experience. Classy women say that those esprits de la pensée also drift through conversations in haute société. Though we were one-for-alls and Semper-Fis, there were times when tension or trouble caused us to fight amongst ourselves. In our psychological stretch-lab both the board and the checkers were in motion, like the insides of a gyroscope.

You could also tell much about a guy from his *irregular* name—nicknames gave their personality heft and meaning, nicknames tracked the ascent of their character. My own checkerboard examinations told me that Bay Brother was really the softest, kindest one of us, Zorro the most gifted in painting and drawing (next to me) and the most vicious. In my estimation, Zorro was a born killer and Parrot a natural born slave—anxious to please, to imitate, to follow. Domino and LeMarcus thought in three-sixties, in spheres of influences, as military commanders poised to wallop the enemy of the day.

So there you have the picture, LeMarcus on the perimeter of our checker session, Zorro drawing sketches of Bay Brother getting his checkerboard-butt whipped by Domino, me watching like a low-grade psychologist, and Parrot off fetching somebody's bamboo gun. Speaking of bamboo guns, they all went into the deepest of hiding places when the school bell rang. Bamboo guns have a way of taking on a life of their own, especially at the most inopportune time.

Around about this time my truancy kicked in, quite gradually at first. I admired Zorro's drawing ability; he could draw and crayon just about anything or anybody. Characters just seemed to spring to the page right from under his fingers and his graffiti was at once gripping and hilarious! Favorite teachers riding atop the most outlandish cocks—vaginas as wheeled hot rods with the whole basketball team inside! I won't say anything about bestiality, but his cartoons along those lines made our impromptu gatherings the envy of Beale Street. Anyway, around this time I started imitating Zorro and tried my hand at graffiti and collecting feathers (my way of saving birds). My feather collecting was something I did off and on, nothing real serious. Once I had come under my Master's—under Afri's—tutelage, I became more focused on that part and devoted a little more effort to learning which feathers came from certain birds. I didn't discuss my new apprenticeship with any of my gang members, *Tell some and keep some,* I said to myself. Our name, Las Siestas, meant nap as in sleep —but we twisted that and used it for nap as in hair, 'cause we loved both sleep and hair. That way the name tied things up. We also adopted Domino's motto, All-for-One, as our own. Occasionally, we would roam around the areas of south Memphis, out to Fort Pickering and beyond. Ghetto rumor has it that if you ever see a river rat in Memphis, you might want to protect your dog and bring a gun more potent than one made from bamboo. We ended up testing that rumor; it became an interesting sidebar to my tale.

  Now as I scribe these revelations—invisible, archetypal footfalls etched in the stained glass windows of memory—I smell repetitions, taste seasonings that suggests a diseased rapport, ancient and unequal. Our gangland gusto betrayed a clash of culture lurking in the hallways of society, at once humane and haughty. Our gangland gusto sensed ancient tapestries of decision making afoot, mediation imperiled betwixt tribe and treasurer. Had secretaries of institutions in the arts, religions, and education, lost and bereft in a sea of anxieties, forgotten their ministry; had ministers of institutions in the arts, religion and education, lost and bereft in a sea of anxieties, forgotten their secretaries? When guns and science speak, the arts and creativity must flow, lest both sovereignty and magic suffer...but I digress and get ahead of myself.

III

The gleam on the Brinks Gallery's corridors sparkled, chirping with footfalls of masked patrons attending the Gallery's Petite Masked Ball. New pieces created by local artists—both young and old—and chosen through unique Internet polling and on-site voting, studded gallery walls with statements colorful and bold. The new collection featured works by a cross section of ethnicities in the Memphis community, fired to artistry by the urgencies of their ghettos. Under the rotunda of the art gallery the floor's gleam danced past hand-puppets swathed in the reds and greens of Russian peasants, past Venetian masks chosen to augment a sense of communal mystery, past waiters and waitresses smartly attired and trained to favor the liquid needs of celebrities, and under musicians honoring a request to accompany a folktale chosen to illumine ancient energies between folk and classical art. Once the gleam had pierced the souls of quacking and full throated guests, it gathered gossip and tethered joyfulness to the Friday evening's festivities.

Ramona Giovanelli gallivanted amongst the group saying, Hello Linda, my, you look marvelous. I must get that diet recipe from you, or, Tommy, I am so glad you came—we must chat soon, and various other quaint niceties to her guests. And they were hers because of the detailed arrangements she'd made to cultivate their companionship, hers because of her commitment to artistic understanding, and hers because this anniversary celebration of her directorship built upon this concept: emphasize the rapport between folk and classical art to the breadth of the Memphis community. The idea of a Masked Ball sizzled—a Petite Masked Ball—with Venetian masks, waltzes punctuated with hip-hop, hors d'oeuvres, and a free exhibition of fresh artworks. In her brief greeting to Afri Walker, she said, There are a ton of heavy hitters from the deep pockets of Memphis to make this fun! He surmised that she could recognize the deepest of pockets even with masks on. Talk later, she said smiling. Ramona reveled in strengthening the spiritual cords between the business, political and artistic communities; she abhorred the demise of local support for the classical arts, especially the symphony. Yes, of course sports are important, she said in her welcome statement to the crowd, And the spirit of physical competition is likewise so, but ideas rule paramount and the arts braid both past and future to us in ideas sounded in music, painted in art, and plaited in words.

And the community had responded, recommending high schoolers and collegians who dabbled, old-timers who made art as a hobby or in their spare time, and professional outcasts who became frustrated with the juried classicism of art regulators and left Memphis, prospecting for richer climes. She said, Art brings together our communities and invites immigrants and minorities to enjoy our culture in ways that encourage learning and participation. We can bump and grind right alongside a graceful waltz! Tonight take a casual walk through our gleaming corridors, browse the works chosen by the public of our first annual Folkways competition, feast your eyes on the glories of our new Community wing. Her heart had experienced the long, fading screech of art dying at the hands of business persons privatizing ensembles and stalking artists with starvation diets. Art lives in Memphis and Memphis thrives through art, she said, toasting at the end of her short speech. Trained as an artist and knowledgeable in artistic enterprise, Ramona was well aware of the business disposition that arrogantly spun art's creation and presentation around profit principles and delivery efficiencies. Her strategy was to emphasize ancient connections between folk and classical art, to bring ancient principles of community, folk and classical art interstices, and movement through dance. Long live artistic merit through this new avenue of presentation! she said. In the corner a string quartet had tuned, playing a series of bright waltzes, joined by a sprightly clarinetist.

Sir?—said a nearby waiter. The word broke the stare of one of the presenting artists examining a group of hand puppets dangling from a puppet stand close to the museum store. The puppets were comically fashioned in garments of old Russian peasants, serfs and royalty. Can I interest you in a glass of wine? said the waiter. I'm sorry, oh-oh yes, thank you. That would be nice, said the artist, nattily attired in a checkered shirt, dark suit and loafers. White or red sir? said the waiter. Pinot Grigio if you have it, said the artist.

Marvelous choice! said another voice to the artist, as the waiter handed the artist white wine in a plastic cup. This voice that struck the artist ear was deeper, and cultured in an accent steeped in open vowels. The Voice came from behind a Gotham-inspired Greek mask that glittered with silverish-gold. We have not been formally introduced, but I couldn't pass up this opportunity to congratulate you on your piece—MemNoire. It's a splendid addition to this intrepid new wing. The mask, angled at its most oblique, stood atop a steel-gray suit, with eyes both searching and confident. It is a bold experiment for our pedestrian and traditional Brinks, continued the Voice-of-Gotham. From its position of prominence and clever use of dappled color, I would define you as a disciple of Jackson Pollack—yes, I see palpable parallels in your use of color and pattern, and tinged I might add with El Greco—that elongated figure of a medieval chapel with a church bell perched above. A remarkable contrast to all that abstract expressionism —mystic ardor. But, I couldn't help noticing—there is no value, no price on your work! Such a pity.

The artist extended his hand and said, Afri Walker here and you?—Me?—most unimportant, Voice-of-Gotham said and continued, I take it that you interposed a church bell or two rummaging around in that dark din of a sky that, perhaps, is Memphis? And taken a step further that this medieval bell should ring for a special day—perhaps the birthday of Martin King? The artist stood mask-free, proud that his work had won a place in the new wing;

the question made him feet a bit off-balance. His short acceptance speech had been designed to thank the powers that be for this opportunity to display his wares; of course, he would grant the gallery permission to display the piece longer, should it so desire. He acknowledged this public display as an arousal to both public conscience and consciousness. *This voice has such robustness in its tenor; could it be one of a singer?*

Well, said Afri, cautiously aware of the eerie silence and constellation of cupped ears standing in close proximity. Between high-heeled ankles that clinked and cupped earlobes that dangled, femme fatals animated this indoor landscape with spangled glitter, peels of laughter, and a wondrous smörgåsbord of shapes, sizes, and skin-tight booty. Many say that to them it does tell a story, continued Afri, And to tell the truth, I think it would have a— Voice-of-Gotham interrupted saying, And you will tell me that art is the angel of peace and culture, art inspires thought through repetition and development —where does this MemNoire repeat and wherefore does it develop? Come now, your MemNoire seeks to serve as a call to invite new membership into the realm of humanity? What is the price for?—Afri countered saying, It is *not* for sale, it has no price! It is designed to honor this new wing and the processes that brought it here my friend. It honors the Memphis Belle, the protector of life and liberty for all Americans. It serves as a bellwether for our youth, especially those of color who see nihilism in their days and anguish in their nights. Its model rests in my studio as a stimulant to professional development. His voice cruised robustly now, echoing in the silence of their heated debate, I see Memphis afresh, inclusive in both history and future, supporting healthy, creative development of all citizens. In my estimation, that occurs through creativity in the arts. Otherwise, folk become psychological cripples—alcoholics, druggies, decrepit misfits! Wheedling, Voice-of-Gotham said, Yet *dollars* floated this wing! Afri shot back saying, The athletic and business communities bulldoze art, they want a cookie cutter culture that cements materialistic hierarchies, ladders grounded in money and physical power, military power. Is that what we are to become?

The man behind the mask took Afri aside by his elbow, steering him away from prying ears. Speaking in low, deliberate tones he said, We have much to discuss about ladders, my friend, but for now, I will offer you five thousand dollars for your MemNoire. Some few nearby and closest in the gathering flinched as they heard the masked man make that offer. A good third of the guests heard the figure and now upwards of half hissed gossip about it. Did you hear that? Jeez, why are they talking about money? He refused the offer! That and other variations on the theme, its repetitions and variations, its development even, sizzled through the crowd. The gossip grew organic, achieving artistry on its own, thriving as art itself.

Needless to say, I'm disappointed, Voice-of-Gotham said tapping Afri on his lapel. Me too, said a buxom brunette standing close by and giggling, I thought he'd love to spend it on me! she said. With lips reddened, overtaken by the comic spirit of a Joker, Voice-of-Gotham said, Think about this as you listen to the puppet show, a petite but powerful representation of the Firebird folktale. Stravinsky put that folktale to music. I think, as a young artist—perhaps overly idealistic—you will appreciate both the story, its implications, its realities, and even its many possible resolutions. Afri said, I have other paintings that you are welcome—Not interested! interjected the Voice adding, The painting I want is like the princess in this folktale, princess Vassilisa who wants her dress—the dress she embroidered—now at the bottom of the blue sea. Here, take this program. It contains the original version of the folktale; *read it*. She wants her dress and will not be dissuaded from her desire. I want that painting though it is not mine. Though I did not create it, by tradition I should be able to purchase, to engage commerce, assign value—By virtue of privilege, said Afri, Birthright and color—is that your point? said Afri.

      Instead of drawing away, the face grew closer. Afri could smell the wine-stink of his breath, the reddish rage of eyes behind the mask. The consonants of Voice-of-Gotham grew crisp as toast, he said, Here's a little variation on this damn folktale. An artist's mind is on a hunt and runs across a bell's clapper. The mind's instinct tells the artist not to touch it as bad things will happen. His mind ignores the advice and brings the clapper back to the artist so that it will be praised and rewarded. When the artist is presented with the clapper he demands the entire bell or the mind will be put to death. The mind weeps to his instinct which tells him to put dollars in the field in order to capture the bell. The bell comes down seeking to chime over those *dead presidents,* enabling the mind to capture the bell. Now, that's a funky synopsis of the story, a bleak variation on a small portion, but you get my drift. That corn is dollars, *dead presidents!* Are you absolutely sure that MemNoire is not for sale! hissed Voice-of-Gotham. Not, said Afri icily, for sale!

     Warm-up sounds of strings, a variety of drumming sounds, and of clarinet arpeggios tinkered above crowd-noise. Afri sailed across the room in long strides and took a conspicuous seat near the front so as to disengage his masked storyteller. Once again, he found himself entranced by the remarkable colors and patterns of the hand puppets and reflected on the folktale, murky in his memory. He challenged himself to read the program rolled in his fist later. Ramona quietly slipped into a chair next to him, and whispered, I almost came over to you and Hargrove to see what the ruckus was all about. Did you guys argue? Afri said, Hargrove?—so that's his name—he was disappointed by my answer, I'll tell you about it. Don't know if this show will work, says Ramona, I didn't get a chance to see the rehearsal. A narrator approached the front of the puppet stage as the gathering settled in their seats and Afri made mental notes on a ravishing puppet princess dressed in greens, golds, and reds, a stately king crowned in silver and purples, and an ardent, well-armored prince astride a proud stallion.

And now my friends, said the narrator in tones of a circus master, Welcome to our rendition of this famous Russian folktale, made international by Diaghilev and Igor Stravinsky. For our concert, Stravinsky's score has been chiseled and arranged by clarinetist Fergus Baptiste of the Memphis Philharmonic. *Fergus Baptiste, Hey, thought Afri, I know that name.* He is joined by violinist Jan Compton and pianist Hosea Gillian. Welcome to our marriage of folk art to classical art, to music on and at the Brinks. The lighting captured the small puppets on the stage and murmurs in the crowd diminished as the music began.

The ensemble of musicians started with a slow, chromatic passage in lower ranges of both clarinet and piano with the princely archer on horseback, searching for food and treasure. What a marvelous plume I see in the distance, said the archer. Immediately, the violin and clarinet supported the action with jocular articulations in the piano. Harmony typical of Stravinsky colored the escapade. Don't touch it, cried the horse, as bad things will happen. The archer ignores the horse, gathers the feather and presents it to the king. Instead of praise and reward, the archer is threatened with death by King Kastchei. The archer is ordered to bring the entire bird to the king. Prominently displaying the king's mood, insistent rhythms permeate the ensemble joined by percussive rolls on the conga drum, as the king throws a monumental tantrum. The archer puppet weeps to his horse and says, What on earth shall I do? and the horse replies, Spread *corn* on the open field. The bird will come down to eat and you can capture it. After capturing the bird, the archer triumphantly presents it to King Kastchei. The march orchestrated by Baptiste captures this moment, in music strikingly similar to Prokofiev's Peter and the Wolf. The puppet king, still indignant, proposes another challenge to the archer under threat of death. Still whispering, Ramona says, The clarinetist did a marvelous adaptation, don't you think? Afri nodded agreement. The orchestra performed the Firebird Suite just last week at the Cannon Center, whispers Ramona. Afri, his mind remotely lingering on Voice-of-Gotham (Hargrove) hears *corn* in the dialog and thinks, *its corn not coin, fool—Hargrove!* Fetch!—bellows the king—the princess Vassilisa to me, the one famous for her embroidery and lives in the far-off land. I wish to marry her! Once again the archer weeps to his horse; together they execute a plan to drug the princess. On awakening after her capture, Vassilisa sings a long lament, echoed in clarinet and piano and embellished in a lush violin ostinato. I am so unhappy, says the princess. So far away from my homeland, family and friends, so distant from the tools of my embroidery. If I am to be married, at least let me be dressed in my own creation embroidered by my own hands.

    A thunderous roll sounds in the deepest of conga drums, followed by leaping arpeggios in the violin, as the narrator issues rhyme verbalized as rap, with a repetitive percussion, a la rap music. I just took a sip of counterfeit, it wasn't a lot just a little bit.

Thought it was a party so I didn't quit, Drank too much now here I sit! sang the narrator. The gathering roared its approval, whistling and clapping as though it were a jazz concert. Ordered yet again to fetch, the archer retrieves the dress, hidden under a rock in the deep blue sea; even with her dress the princess suffers in happiness. She demands a boiling of the prince in hot water. Trapped in this dilemma, the archer weeps again to his horse. Here the music sounds again, skipping off in asymmetrical rhythms more akin to Messiaen than Stravinsky, and eliciting a smile from Ramona. The archer comes out more handsome than ever, dressed as a young prince. In jealous rage, the king imitates the boiling scene and is boiled to death and the prince and princess are married, living happily ever after.

Following repeated bows of the puppets, narrator, and musicians, Ramona thanks the crowd, lauds the musicians and says, Ladies and Gentlemen. Thank you for your presence and your enthusiasm. We could not have accomplished this step without your participation and support. Please share your thoughts with us and thank our board members as you exit. Follow us on Twitter, Facebook and the Internet. Dear reader, for your information I herewith share the program's version of the Firebird Folktale:

The Firebird and Princess Vassilisa.
In this version a king's archer is
on a hunt and runs across a firebird's
feather. The archer's horse warns the archer
not to touch it, as bad things will happen. The

archer ignores the advice and takes it to bring back to the king so he will be praised and rewarded. When the king is presented with the feather he demands the entire firebird or the death of the archer. The archer weeps back to his horse who instructs him to put corn on the fields in order to capture the firebird. The firebird comes down to eat allowing the archer to capture the bird. When the king is presented with the firebird he demands the archer fetch the Princess Vassilisa so the king may marry her, otherwise the archer will be killed. The archer goes to the princess's lands and drugs her with wine to bring her back to the king. The king was pleased and rewarded the archer, however when the princess awoke and realized she was not home she began to weep. If she was to be married she wanted her wedding dress, which was under a rock in the middle of the Blue Sea. Once again the archer wept to his horse and fulfilled his duty to his king and brought back the dress. The princess was stubborn and refused to marry the king even with her dress until the archer was dipped in boiling water. The archer begged to see his horse before he was boiled and the horse put a spell on the archer to protect him from the water. The archer came out more handsome than anyone had ever seen. The king saw this and jumped in as well but was instead boiled alive. The archer was chosen to be king and married the princess and they lived happily.

IV

The chirp of footfalls pervasive at the evening's beginning diminished in stark measure as party goers wobbled and stumbled to their cars with masks atop dimmed craniums, arms around newly met waists, slurred voices disappearing into darkness, and the sparkled gleam on the floor now gone. Afri Walker made way to his Honda down the front steps of the Brinks Gallery, reflective in mood of the evening's festivities. Oh Mr. Walker—just a minute, said someone sliding through the door behind him, You'll be the talk of the town, the pride of the morning's newspaper! It was a female voice, proudly pitched from the mouth of a glittered blond; she tottered unmasked in short clipped steps. I heard you say your piece was not for sale! I think you made that gentleman quite angry when you explained your reasons for keeping it off the market, but I *so* understand your actions. Here, take my card and don't hesitate to call me soon if you change your mind. Thank you ma'am, said Afri taking the card and placing it in his breast pocket, I do appreciate that. I look forward to hearing from you, she added turning to walk to her car. As his eyes tracked her path, he noticed the sheen of that now familiar gray suit standing in the gallery's foyer, its Venetian mask in the Gotham style craned in his direction, its reddened eyes seeming as close as they earlier had been.

Afri resurrected—*its corn not coin, fool!*

Hargrove—as he opened his car door; he considered, scissored, and submitted the thought to past experience, past study and mentors, to his subconscious. For many youth in Memphis, the avenues of exposure to international culture were named limited and non-existent. Established cultural institutions had made meager inroads in minority communities. Prevailing establishment attitudes suggested that masterworks and prominent antiquities reveal their greatness as self-evident. Knee-jerk reactionaries in minority communities, especially those of African-American descendants rejected classical art, finding its supporters dictatorial in their steadfast refusal to expand it canon to influences outside the dominant culture. In short, they would not have their cultural menus dictated by the tastes of conservative boards of directors. *That corn is dollars, dead presidents.* Minority critiques underlined the obvious shortage of works by South American and African American creative artists programmed in the homeland. Historical shortages of works translated into shortage of support, into shortage of new works and ultimately into dialogue hell. The result: shallow programming by orchestras to encourage and support African-Americans composers. Ditto for galleries. Limited productivity, interpreted as inferior ability, left lingering the ghosts of intellectual superiority. This stunted dialogue, racist and historically unnatural on both sides, rendered classical and folk art stale and strangely irrelevant. The populist line, even of the commonwealth, read: give us your dollar or get out!

The desperate state of arts education available to urban youngsters ignited culture wars, rendering established cultural institutions across the city financially unstable, flagging in popularity. Questions crossed Afri's mind. What does it take to bridge the precarious contemporary scene in art? How can I fit my vision, use my training to wrestle fresh masterworks expressing my vision from popular, folk, and classical tools? How can you achieve new levels of mastery? He had read biography, carved, read technique, painted, drawn, read art history, sketched copiously, studied steadily with available artists and teachers, traveled widely to experience art works, and given himself over to the physical trials and intellectual trails of those who grew as he wished to grow. A variation of the folktale he'd heard tempted him with a substitution.

An artist's ego is on a hunt and runs across a firebird's feather. The ego's horse warns the ego not to touch it, as bad things will happen. The ego ignores the advice and takes it to bring back to the artist so it will be praised and rewarded. When the artist is presented with the feather he demands the entire firebird or the death of the ego.

Though humorous, he found some consolation in this small portion. He had found submersion of the ego important, especially in the learning, and lessons in life are to be learned each day. Yes, ego must be submerged to aid learning. Bit by bit, test by test, he drew closer to his goal: mastery. Along the way, he had not only drawn closer to realizing his vision of a work; he became closer to mastering both his tools and himself. *From time to time, the ego must be dipped in boiling water!* What is mastery—define it! he heard himself demand...*comprehensive knowledge and skill in a subject or accomplishment, with ego dipped in boiling water!* His own laughing voice spun around the car's cabin meeting his face with a smile. Instead of making a left turn on Danny Thomas, he continued on Poplar making a left on Front Street. The bell statue, sliced from the entire instrument, and resident at the Center's corner was a grim reminder that its progenitor, the saxophone, was rarely present in classical music concerts. He headed down to view the Mississippi, refusing further consideration of the lopsided meander of current musical tastes.

     Upon reaching Tom Lee Park, he made a right, slowly pulling to a stop, and surveyed the broad expanse of the Mississippi River and took in watery reflections of the bridge and the mighty quiet of its muffled roar. The fund drive for the new wing of the gallery had been a contentious one. Diverse members of the community had long argued for a more equitable representation of contemporary art, art reflecting the experiences of the battle for human rights initiated and fought by the African American community. Those arguments caught the city fathers off guard, leaving skirmishers counterpoised between the exhale of Martin King's death and the inhale of developing next steps. A photo exhibit of the strike by garbage workers had placated the skirmishers in small degree, but commissions of works for and about the struggle by African-Americans, by women, by Hispanics, was yet forthcoming. The discussion had been aired in print media, blossoming to include all cultural institutions in Memphis—the symphony, the zoo, the library, churches, schools, theaters, movie houses, and resulting in calls for broadened attention to the intellectual needs of diverse minorities locally on one side, and increased financial giving by those same diverse minorities on the other. The *Give us your (last) dollar or get out! That pseudo-commonwealth crap again!*

Diversity of ideas, especially where black minorities were concerned, meant attention to divergent strains of accommodation and militancy in the black community. The black minority's fight to end slavery and Jim Crow challenged democracy's commitment to human rights. For conservative, old guard Memphis, this was a problem. Many conservatives felt that minorities did not support old guard institutions—the symphony, the zoo, the library, churches, schools, theaters, movie houses—financially, except through taxes. In the recent past two institutions, the zoo and the library, had made notable efforts towards increased diversity coupled with eclecticism. Those institutions had also prospered. The Folkways Community wing at the Brinks was its response to criticism that Brinks was anchored in the past, boring in its holdings, and recalcitrant in its forward intellectual movement. The success of the Civil Rights Museum in Memphis countered claims that black history, and its corollary artistic vitality would be unprofitable. Sports-minded Memphis, initially slow to learn embrace diversity, now basked in the glow of basketball profitability. The newly resurrected mantra of the twentieth century became once again, may the best man win!

Art historians, scholars, and academicians felt that folk art for the new wing should be chosen by jury. Community leaders and some members of the board of directors felt that pieces for this wing should be chosen by Internet polling and on-site voting. The formula ultimately chosen to guide selections was held as a closely guarded secret and revealed as a functional success. During the process, Civil War generalities, dated prejudices, and moribund psychologies were exposed and aired with regularity. Ramona had navigated a compromise that embraced both classical and folk art establishments and mathematically developed a selection formula which incorporated both views. Into that void stepped Walker and his MemNoire; if controversy followed, he would ride the cusp of the Brinks. Just as he cranked the engine to finish his drive home (his apartment occupied the upstairs floor of the studio) his cell phone rang. Hey, he said noting the name Ramona on the screen, Whassup!

Afri you were a big hit with MemNoire tonight. I had a ton of compliments on the exhibit, but your piece got wonderful comments—the press will carry a nice story soon and they want to interview you. I'll stop by your studio in the next day or so to show you some comments made by visitors and by the board. If I forgot to say so, congratulations! Thank you very much Ramona—your support has meant a lot, especially over these past few weeks, said Afri. Have a great night and stop by whenever you can. Congratulations to you for escaping that mean crossfire that's been in the press! Bye now. He made a smooth turn onto Riverside Drive; the specter of the Memphis Bridge now in his rear-view mirror. He hummed gently as he drove; Watchin' the tide roll away, ooh I'm sittin' on the dock of the bay—and reached for the CD itself, playing Otis as he headed for home. He guided the Honda down to West Carolina, turned onto Main Street, parked on the east side of the street, and smiled to himself thinking of his need for an apprentice. *Need to get a CD of that Firebird Suite, maybe two. I used to have a cassette of that thing, but it would be nice to have two or three to compare orchestras; he made a mental note.* He had several new ideas for his next piece and knew the style he wanted to portray—*maybe the subject would declare that it be a sculpture instead of a painting like MemNoire.* Or, maybe it would be a painting first and then haunt him until he did it as a sculpture. Anyway, he needed some help around the studio—somebody that would be dependable and maybe even with a bit of talent. M3, the bell that he had fashioned had turned out to be a huge pain to finish.

He had studied the process of creating a bronze sculpture and watched the process applied on several YouTube videos—but watching someone else create a work of art and doing it yourself are two different things. He said to himself, You can do that, if the ancients can do it, then you can too! He'd broken the steps down and drawn several models—really, sketches—of how he wanted M3 to look and measure. Afri had created a decent clay model of the thing and dug out a fairly large sand pit in the floor of the studio. He'd even gone so far as to paste the steps on the wall. The work had been backbreaking and if he was to be successful in the pour—the step that he'd screwed up previously in that manufacturing step—he would need some help. He needed extra hands to pull off the pouring step if he tackled that kind of operation again. What would you even look for in a helper? he asked himself. How would you choose such a person? Maybe you should get someone experienced in that step? How will you know if the person is trustworthy? Maybe you need someone you can teach yourself? Perhaps it would be better to take a course in bronze casting—after all, your own apprenticeship was essentially in painting and art history! The last thing you need is someone you can't trust, *a rattlesnake in your pocket.* Perhaps a female, maybe get some recommendations from Ramona. In the end, he decided to put off thinking about all that; it had been a long day and a fairly long night. He turned the key on the iron facade at his studio's entrance, entered the wooden door, locking both after entry, quick-scanned the studio, climbed the stairs up to his personal quarters, stripped himself of clothing, brushed his teeth and slipped into bed. Wow, I am really tired, he thought and turned in for the night.

V

For me, perplexed as I was about the business of school, grunting as an unofficial member of Las Siestas made me more comfortable. I had a magical array of excuses about my apathy: I had no loving dad in the house, I needed a mentor, my learning style was more hands on—I needed auto mechanics and woodshop, *reading made me sleepy*, I hated the subject, I *weren't nobody's slave,* can't nobody tell me what to do, my teacher wasn't my momma (or daddy)—all the crap you hear from kids intent on performing at the lowest possible level (you hear that one from girls too nowadays). Las Siestas had me all pumped up about their escapades—who they screwed, who they whipped, who they had it in for, who they would jump. Experience proved that their stories turned out to be mostly lies. The one about slavery—ain't nobody's slave—was one that got mumbled a lot around school. The one about slaves—ain't nobody's slave—was the one that tickled me the most, since they harassed and ordered people around all the time, for the heck of it. Seemed to me like they wanted other folks to be their slaves but didn't want to be one themselves—fetch this, pick up that, kick this person's butt, show this person who is boss. Whenever they would press me about joining the gang, I said, I'm thinking about it, which itself was a lie since I wasn't thinking at all; my grades were a testament to that. Like I said, my mom had set me up with that computer reading program and read to me a lot, folktales, mythologies, religious stories, and other stories too about gifted African Americans.

I ambled down Main Street on this particular day with my mind in my pocket, my hat on backwards and a can of yellow spray paint. I'd seen Zorro draw some awesome graffiti objects with hands underneath, you know, like a presentation or somethun'. Determined as I was to show them I had Gangsta Grit and South Memphis Swag, I sauntered up to a virgin concrete wall and cut loose with a bright yellow crown—the kind that you see decorated with Cornbread Be King, and put a huge hand, with fingers and all, handing to the great out-of-doors! That was when I heard Afri (I didn't know his name then), hands on his hips, saying, Bring some of that energy over here boy, you look like you need a job and I need an apprentice! You interested? I stood there, mouth agape, wondering how to answer that question and said, Depends. Tell you what, he said stepping quickly into the gated door of a two story building, read this to me out loud, it's a folktale about—well you'll find out. That was the extent of the test he manufactured for me. Maybe manufactured is not quite the right word, improvised is better, 'cause it felt like he thought it up on the spot.

Understand that my homies, soon to be fellow Siestas, read like lead was on the tip of their tongues—whatever words stood in front of them came out in forms and shapes unfathomable to modern man. Consonants got mangled and brutalized, syllables became ambushes, and sentences got split into parts and pieces rent asunder losing any semblance of continuity—that is all except for LeMarcus. I won't mention grade level, but while the rest of the country was knee-deep in *programming* for computers, for them, a *sentence* was closely akin to swimming across the Mississippi. And they wanted me to join up with them and put up with their initiation crap—Jeez! Talk about slavery, the trials and tribulations they thought up for recruits would make slavery look like a walk in the park, or so I reckoned.

How much you gone pay me? I said when this fella came back. He handed me a program with the part I was supposed to read circled in red and said, That depends lil brother on how well you read. Now with the passage of time, I have run across one other fellow that took on this job after Afri and I parted ways—not really under the best of circumstances, and she mentioned that The Maestro (that was his newly minted moniker) had devised this two-way deal called dialogue journaling that he laid on them. Actually, he did things a bit differently later, calling this new contract a legal apprenticeship. And that is indeed what I think I should talk about. Don't cha know I did it again—getting ahead of myself I mean; I have just got to learn to stay focused on the issue at hand. Anyway, I read out loud to him, and he said, Excellent—that's not bad, not bad at all. In hindsight, I understand that on a rational level why he took that approach (but on an irrational level, in my gut, I knew the same dilemma existed), with reading being a defining difference between slavery and apprenticeship.

In this version a king's slave/apprentice is on a hunt and runs across a firebird's feather. The slave/apprentice's horse warns the slave/apprentice not to touch it, as bad things will happen. The slave/apprentice ignores the advice and takes it to bring back to the king so he will be praised and rewarded. When the king is presented with the feather he demands the entire firebird or the death of the slave/apprentice. The slave/apprentice weeps back to his horse who instructs him to put corn on the fields in order to capture the firebird. The firebird comes down to eat allowing the slave/apprentice to capture the bird. When the king is presented with the firebird he demands the slave/apprentice fetch the Princess Vassilissa so the king may marry her, otherwise the slave/apprentice will be killed. The slave/apprentice goes to the princess's lands and drugs her with a wine to bring her back to the king. The king was pleased and rewarded the slave/apprentice, however when the princess awoke and realized she was not home she began to weep. If she was to be married she wanted her wedding dress, which was under a rock in the middle of the Blue Sea. Once again the slave/apprentice wept to his horse and fulfilled his duty to his king and brought back the dress. The princess was stubborn and refused to marry the king even with her dress until the slave/apprentice was dipped in boiling water. The slave/apprentice begged to see his horse before he was boiled and the horse put a spell on the slave/apprentice to protect him from the water. The slave/apprentice came out more handsome than anyone had ever seen. The king saw this and jumped in as well but was instead boiled alive. The slave/apprentice was chosen to be king and married the princess and they lived happily.

Me and my homies did not understand the difference between an apprentice and a slave, always jawing about, I ain't no slave, half-stepping in our learnin' while we shoulda been breaking our butts to get lessons. Bay Brother wanted to be just like those drunks waiting for work over a burn barrel in the wintertime; he said so out loud, get to ride around on the back of pickup trucks, drink wine, smoke a blunt. Zorro had said, I gone get me a ride and scooch it up, so I can take my b—ch to college and pick her up after class! We approached school like it was slavery rather than an apprenticeship or a preparation for creativity, for self-guided learning at a higher level. Five bucks an hour, seven max, he said. Okay, I said.

In the early days of my employ, I gained experience just watching how this artist works in his studio. Just watching was a revelation, but my main job consisted of two things: sweeping and dusting. He gave me a list of things to do: dusting, sweeping (there was plenty of sawdust around), sanding (he planned to varnish that pine box), and more dusting (dust flew around that place like a swarm of mosquitoes). Sometimes in the morning we would bong that church bell as if pledging allegiance; for a good while it stood right in front of a huge black and white photo of featherbells. Right in the beginning he had asked me my name. So my friend, what do you call yourself, he asked. I hesitated, aware that I had a variety of nicknames, most of which I hated. He picked up on this and said, Since I found you in the street and you did so well reading that tale about archers and princesses, I dub thee Urchin, prince of the streets. Urchin, I said to myself thinking that it had something to do with church; Granny always admonished me to be a church regular and employ the golden rule, so I felt honored.

    An article appeared in the local paper about the party at the Brinks Gallery and the opening of the new wing. It hailed the opening as a big step for Memphis and congratulated the gallery on its secret formula for selecting new exhibit pieces, saying the formula merited dancing in the streets! We enjoyed a chuckle at that statement, knowing that dancing in the streets in Memphis could be a deadly enterprise. Afri teased, Hey Urchin, if dancing in the streets could bring fractious rapport between races in Memphis then by all means let the Ball begin, give us that salt and pepper boogie on Memphis boulevards! The first paragraph applauded the puppet show and music giving major props to Fergus Baptiste. For Master Afri (he was yet to be dubbed Maestro), the review of MemNoire was not kind. The review read like this:

    Highly touted amongst selectees chosen for the fresh exhibit was a work by Afri Walker, a native of Memphis, with several international credits to his pedigree. His work pays homage to the now famous works of Jackson Pollack and echoes treatments reminiscent of El Greco. Corpulent pools of doodles, scribbles, and veined rivulets cascade about this work charged with abstract intensity. Radiant spools of light yawn from a lone church bell, impotent in attempts to pierce an irreverent darkness. I found this piece vacuous and artistically disturbing for an artist of his experience. Its clever technique masks a message made muddy in mucilage and muck. Other pieces in the exhibit displayed flashes of talent, yet as a group fail to compete with the masterworks found in the traditional gallery. That said, I thank the Board of Directors for this spacious addition to city architecture designed to augment excitement in those portions of our community apathetic towards traditions found in classical masterworks of antiquity. Memphis has much to gain, should these acorns of effort ripen into coin of marketable value.

    My Master had a decidedly strange look on his face when I looked up from my reading. Well Urchin, that says it all, he said, obviously searching for words appropriate to his emotions. That review deserves a frame! and he proceeded to affix it nude to the wall with a nail, frame-less. Nervous regarding my next steps, I turned my attention to practicing the various exercises he'd given me to improve my sense of perspective and accuracy in drawing. I traced my hand, both left and right, made sketches of flowered featherbells on the wall in reverse and upside down, tried drawing without taking my eyes off the objects, worked on sketching with my left hand, and copied hands in anatomy books in various states of translucence; bone, muscle, skeleton, and circulatory systems. Master Afri gave me a hand in my chores, sweeping, dusting, and performing general cleaning.

Once accomplished, he began work on a voluminous series of drawing feathers, saying, I love these feathers that you are collecting Urchin. Where do you find these? I answered, Oh every once in a while I walk through the grounds at the Ornamental Metal Museum—especially the portion that winds through French Fort and Fort Pickering Park—I find feathers of all kinds there.

I could see that Master Afri was enraged by that review, especially the *acorns of effort* part. Time to get to work, he said. I thought, if that wasn't work you just did, then I was confused about those aching muscles I get sometimes, and said, Do you have a new project? No, not entirely—I do have an idea I want to explore, and he fastened his passions onto sketching and drawing different parts of bird anatomy —feathers, heads, legs and toes, wings, each and every anatomical part. It was fascinating to see him draw the part and then start to turn it around in different angles and start to draw all over again, the same part. Whenever he was pleased with a drawing, he went over and rang that bell—BONG! The bell had been his first effort at casting; apparently he made many errors. Urchin, he said, If I do another casting of anything, I will need your help. I couldn't quite pull off that bell by myself, and then he started stalking the studio like he was a football coach on the sidelines, chasing his vision he called it. He showed me some Internet pages he had printed on bird anatomy and said, First draw the bone Urchin,
then the skeleton and its muscles, add the tendons, then the veins and the skin. It's like a recipe. Now

reverse the order. With practice adding and subtracting, building bridges between skin, and bone—and everything in between—I made great strides in my technique.

My friends at school occasionally asked, Where do you make off to after school? Mainly because I high-tailed it out of there to avoid Las Siestas, but they taunted me with weird looks and Zorro sailed paper airplanes my way with cartoons of me steam pressed by an asphalt roller. Occasionally, I felt a navy bean pelt me on the neck, but they didn't jack me up, at least not yet. Urchin, Master Afri would say now and then, How many ways can we look at that folktale? How many questions can we ask about it? How can we reinvent it—subtract, add, multiply, and divide these words—what about substitutions? If we make the King a Critic, we might get a really funny result! He liked to speculate out loud like that. Some of my teachers had talked about acrostics and we had sung rap songs and made poems about summer adventures. Well Master highlighted these words—*Its clever technique masks a muddy message. acorns of effort ripen into coin of marketable value*—and we made up a little ditty to capture its spirit:

A standing ovation captures in time,
If your hard work is worth a dime,
When the critic words come into view,
They blaze as shards that run you through.
Muddy message masked and clever,
Ignited with a Firebird's feather.

Urchin, I think that fellow, that ass-h--- who wrote that review is the same guy that bid on my MemNoire at the Brinks Gallery party. That clown is pissed off cause I wouldn't sell it! Yep, that is the self-same person: Hargrove. Dude wanted to buy that painting—offered me five, no seven thousand dollars for it; jive turkey! Gray-suited Voice of Gotham! He shouted. Now I was starting to really get into my gig; starting to get the smell of paint and the choke of dust into my blood. The BONG of M3 would make the walls of that studio shimmy and vibrate for Martin and Malcolm. My homies lurked about the path to school like black crows on I-40, waiting for roadkill almost evar-day (that's the way the street-blues singers pronounce it). I could never match his energy, swoon myself into the same sea of sweat that spews from his pores, sculpt and carve into the single digits of night. Even though he was the Master and I the Urchin, I wasn't a slave—not in the sense catcalls by Las Siestas suggested. Here's a variation I concocted that began to infest my person.

The Firebird and Princess Vassilisa.
In this version an artist's slave is on a hunt and runs across a firebird's feather. The slave's horse warns the slave not to touch it, as bad things will happen. The slave ignores the advice and takes it to bring back to the artist so he will be praised and rewarded. When the artist is presented with the feather he demands the entire firebird or the death of the slave.

The slave weeps back to his horse who instructs him to put corn on the fields in order to capture the firebird. The firebird comes down to eat allowing the slave to capture the bird. When the artist is presented with the firebird he demands the slave fetch the Princess Vassilisa so the artist may marry her, otherwise the slave will be killed.

The slave goes to the princess's lands and drugs her with a wine to bring her back to the artist's. The artist was pleased and rewarded the slave, however when the princess awoke and realized she was not home she began to weep. If she was to be married she wanted her wedding dress, which was under a rock in the middle of the Blue Sea. Once again the slave wept to his horse and fulfill his horse before he was boiled and the horse put a spell on him to protect him from the water. The slave came out more handsome than anyone had ever seen. The artist saw this and jumped in as well but was instead boiled alive. The slave was chosen to be artist and married the princess and they lived happily.

VI

Visitors to the new Folkways Community Wing of the Brinks Gallery were treated to a new exhibit last night, said the Memphis NewsBeat. This exhibit threatens to be a formidable addition to the presentation of art in the city of Memphis. The opening, a celebration of new artworks (hopefully masterworks) selected by ingenious and experimental methods, was a combination of many things: social occasion, wine tasting, cheese bar, puppet show, and an exhibit for fresh paintings. This collection displayed new artistic creations yet to be christened masterpieces by juried methods, but selected by popular methods—a kind of people's choice—christened as distinguished representations of mastery by citizens and community polling. A colorful mixture of ethnicities enjoyed this gathering including the Brinks Gallery Board of Directors, prominent citizens, visual artists, patrons, ensembles from the Memphis Philharmonic, blues artists usually ensconced in Beale Street establishments, jazz artists from the University of Memphis, city and county officials, and family and friends of the honorees. The festivities began at 6:00 pm, with the clicks and tinkling of glasses bleating at 7:00 sharp.

Delighted to have been amongst the honorees, thrilled to be in the number, Afri thought. *Wish that my parents could have lived long enough to see me bathe in this moment.* He had been emboldened and buoyed by their respectful and joyful support of his artistic efforts, even a s a child. He had

enjoyed the Stravinsky, loved the puppeteer and hand puppets, and drawn strength from the princess's call for her embroidered dress, for her creative opus lying at the bottom of the sea. He smiled thinking of the creative process animated in the short term by the prince and in the long term by the princess. The phrase, *at the bottom of the sea,* humored him into thinking of that great magical force which causes artists to crawl and grovel through pain and a hardship to give birth to personal vision. *Been there, done that*; and he reflected on his journey to mastery, his own apprenticeship.

As you know Urchin, he said, sidestepping his way around the sand pit, and he fish-eyed his dutiful apprentice with a smirk, An artist should probably never read reviews, but my curiosity just wouldn't let me leave this newspaper alone. Ramona had warned Afri about reading reviews, about trusting the wordy aesthetics of critics and sponsors who clamored as aesthetes, desiring to be creative themselves. Urchin received the comment unceremoniously with face transparent and taciturn in
the style learned watching many checker games. Being naïve and much less sophisticated in art at the time, I had scant knowledge of the anatomy of a review. *Can't show it to nary a partner,* damn, those guys can't even read it, mostly. Urchin decided to throw the situation in reverse, How about you use it for inspiration—you got it tacked on the wall, you can rotate it or throw darts at it—or blow beans at it with

this bamboo gun, and he brought out his bamboo gun from the pocket of his jeans.

Hmm, thought Afri *noetically,* perhaps this new apprentice could be someone who could appreciate mastery and its attendant effort and discipleship after all. Discipleship: that word has religious implications, has galaxies of invisibles orbits that hum and careen around it. And what about the journey of mastery itself, in sports, in music and theater, in painting and sculpture achieved through long reflection, practiced in hours of transpositions and memorizations, of transportations and language learning, of written research in foreign libraries, and of loving collaborations with others of like mind. Mastery, discipleship, creativity, collaboration: those words held the essence of his journey to the Brinks. He reflected on his newfound artfellow The Firebird Suite, a classic which drew inspiration from a folktale; a masterful collaboration of symphonic and Russian folktale, expressed in dance by puppets. His imagination substituted African-American for Russian. *Call Fergus, see if he has a videotape ...what about Ramona?* He wanted to share the puppet show with Urchin, measure his level of commitment, eek out insights into his capacity for growth.

Hey, that's kinda cool, said Afri examining the grain in a hollowed piece of wood with his fingertips. Ramona had spoken to Afri about weird turns a review might take. She'd said, watch out for taking a review too seriously; sometimes a critic doesn't understand the step an artist takes to realize his or her vision, doesn't respond well to a new direction the artist wants to explore. Their phone conversation centered on questions that he now shared with Urchin. Afri said, Okay Urchin, Here are the questions that Ramona thinks are important when a critic hears a concert or attends an exhibit of art. These are the questions that guide her appraisal of an art event! What can I learn from this exhibit? What are the facts of this exhibit? What is the audience response to the music? How do audience members review the exhibit in their emails? Do patrons or critics reveal personal bias or gain in their comments? What aesthetic statements are found in the artwork? Does the reviewer urge the community to judge live, non-digitized performances or exhibits for themselves?

Unused to seeing his Master deep in thought, Urchin said, So Master Afri, what is your reaction to the review—from the sound of it, he did not enjoy your work! Afri tried to keep the same taciturn expression, tried to keep his words well modulated and thoughtful in tone: harmless. To Afri, the words felt apprehensive and tentative. Well Urchin, he said, I suppose that he did not appreciate my perspective on how church bells should look or how they might function. Let me get back to that question once we get some of this dust under control. Plus, I have a game I want to play with you. A game, Urchin said expectantly, hoping to raise his spirits, What game? Look, Afri said in avid response, I did several preparatory sketches—in pencil and charcoal—for MemNoire and some watercolor paintings as trial runs. I also did some research on how critics develop written critiques of an art show. I wanted to be prepared for whatever came my way. Here are the sketches and paintings. Tell me your reactions to—and how you make up your reactions to a piece of art or music.

Urchin answered with extreme hesitancy, wondering more about how Afri would react to his words, than what exact words he would use to make his case. Well Master, he said, if the review urges me to go see the exhibit, that would be a good thing. The symphony has visited my school in the past; we got to learn about the instruments. That bell in the drawings, it looks like it's on the cusp of ringing—in fact, it looks as if it would ring at any moment. If I see these two sketches together, it looks like you are experimenting with colors—how they conflict or harmonize. I like the way the colors are reflected in the bell and in the water in the background.

Exactly, said Afri, and as you examine this painting live, you can step closer to it or father away, examine the textures, play with the angles of perception, just as you could in a concert where the seating was randomized–say—after a movement or the conclusion of a piece! Those things could not happen if the piece were digitized. It's probably more difficult in music, but the same principles apply. Now here is what I propose. I love your idea of using rotation as a means of investigating an idea. I will take one of my paintings—preps for MemNoire, and position it, first as is, then rotated forty five degrees left, ninety degrees left, a hundred and eighty degrees and so on, perhaps mirrored accordingly. I want you to do your own sketches of the piece at those different angles; paint exactly what you see! Then we'll add some color—like—the colors you used on the wall across the street—bold and reckless colors, to see what happens.

You never told me you liked my graffiti, Urchin thought; he said, Okay, you said you saw talent someplace in that mural. One of my friends says that when you do a really good job at something, you can hear the coyote sing deep in your breast. Urchin did several sketches that day and the next, engrossed even as dust thickened beneath his feet. He wondered about the origin of all that dust in the studio and noticed Afri polishing and sanding away on a small oval piece of wood in a far corner. Was it a puppet? A wooden puppet of the kind that you put on some strings? which he sanded and polished every so often. Just as Afri had suggested, Urchin rotated his Master's sketches at the suggested angles. When he finished, he asked, What am I looking for?

Okay, you are looking for something distinctive and positive and...some characteristic that you find in each different rotation. An unusual characteristic that you can tease, play with in the final sketch, the sketch you choose as your model. More than anything, you have taught, trained, learned—with your muscles, arms, fingers and eyes—have refined your ability to coordinate what you see with what you reproduce; you have engaged in achieving exactitude. Afterwards, you get to play with color and light, like the impressionists; where is it dark, gay, lively, heroic, tragic, humorous? You are looking for a unique and compelling way to augment the model sketch you have chosen, just as a composer will announce a piece with the trumpet, echo it in the strings and perhaps mute it with the French horn. All those colors are different and the masters employ them to achieve dramatic effect. As he spoke, his eyes flashed on the review and he read aloud this portion:

Corpulent pools of doodles, scribbles, and veined rivulets cascade about...charged with abstract intensity. Radiant spools of light yawn from a lone church bell, impotent in attempts to pierce an irreverent darkness. I found this piece vacuous and artistically disturbing for an artist of his experience. Its clever technique masks a message made muddy in mucilage and muck. Other pieces in the exhibit displayed flashes of talent, yet as a group fail to compete with the masterworks found in the traditional gallery.

The quiver in his voice, and the jab in his finger revealed a lingering, seething anger. Does that part make you angry? Urchin said, not allowing his eyes to leave his work. Do you have any navy beans? Me, navy beans—? The phone rang and I heard my Master say, Oh no...it's not for sale. He calmly repeated those words several times, as he had done with preceding callers.

Yep, Afri said, navy beans—wait, I may have some, and he popped out and back into the main room in a flash. Beans, Urchin, beans!! While he blew beans at that review, I started in on making my sketches and drawings. It was almost as if he were one of my gang, traipsing along on the way to school, enjoying the walk and looking for little targets to aim at. After all that sweat and searching, tons of fantasizing and investigation of techniques to make a meaningful statement, scouting for combinations of theme, subject and context to make the piece, he was pissed and bitter with a review that made him feel unappreciated.

One of the patrons sent a letter to the newspaper, a letter to the editor, that the newspaper printed later that week. It read as follows:

The Folkways Wing at the Brinks Gallery is a bold experiment to encourage this city's cultural institutions towards inclusion of the creative works of minorities. This effort seeks a fresh balance between customer appeal and creative inclusion. In our not so distant past, Jim Crow stood at the doors of each Memphis cultural institution. Though Jim Crow has been assassinated in the military, the effects of his surly watch yet exist in the churches, schools, artistic venues, and galleries of our fair city. Inclusion must be both active and passive, and above all joyful. In a community sun-baked with illiteracy, what institution has stepped up to the plate in reading, offering face-to-face and web-based support. Our critic seems more of a king than an archer. The words in his quiver bear poison that punishes effort and arraigns imagination. Our critic spurns the artist with the hoots, jeers, and spit formerly reserved for black youth seeking education the high schools of the deep south during the Eisenhower administration. Thank goodness the Board of Directors hashed this thing out, engaged techniques of mediation, and was ably led by Directress Ramona Giovanelli to both build the Wing and initiate a competition of and by the people, which illustrates the dynamism fundamental to the relationship between folk and classical art. We were so close to that balance in music, between folk music (blues, country, popular) at one point in the life of our Memphis Philharmonic. Let us pray that this balance will be restored, with supreme haste.

As I write now, I remember phone calls of congratulations, flowers, and art agents calling the studio asking to speak with Maestro Walker. *Critic seems more of a king than an archer: wow, like a king ordering folks around! To the writer of that letter, the critic almost seemed jealous of the creative acumen of the artist.* My master, previously aggrieved and in horrific emotional disarray, sat sketching and blowing navy beans at the review itself, now starting to show signs of wear and tear: bean-bushed! To my surprise, he showed me a new sketch, one made in ink with one of my quills. The sketch, a menacing likeness of a huge bird, feathers nervous and agitated like the quills of a demonic porcupine, stood in the center of the page in permanent rage over a large round globe. A new idea? I said meekly, already visualizing a firebird swirling in tornadic color. Aha Urchin, he said, Your questions are an inspiration. Several new projects; one for a friend, here's a sample puppet head for you, and a bamboo gun for me! Can you make another without too much trouble? I nodded in the affirmative. Splendid Urchin, splendid! Oh yeah, he added, And a new bird of fire! Just picked up some new mojo Urchin, some brand new mojo! You know, there are all kinds of mafias that try to nip you in the butt. Time to move on, get to the next stage, let MemNoire take care of itself. But keep it under your hat Urchin...under thy hat my man, no word, no mention. I have seen physical effort inspired by physical challenge on a basketball court and football field. I have never seen the sweat, perspiration, and sheer energy inspired by this one sketch of hawk-like bird, unbridled on a page of parchment. I stuffed that precious parchment in my shoulder bag. Over the next few months, I would join the ranks of initiates to the *effort* of artistic endeavor.

VII

The new mojo that flowed in the veins of my Master washed us deep into the night, with me dusting, sweeping, sanding, scrubbing, and occasionally drawing and practicing those exercises that he'd laid out for me. Afri chiseled and sketched with the fury of an attack dog I'd seen on TV. I'd slept on a palette that he'd shellacked for my use and woke up only once to use the room of release. Though my rest was calm (I awoke the next day with the lines on my body suggesting lack of movement), I remembered that I had dreamed of a snake but the memory was hazy and squishy! Had I stepped on or eluded the snake? I'd thought of trying to make the trip to Granny's place, but on Friday night Las Siestas might be roaming about; I had not seen them for many days and suspected that they might act on their curiosity to ferret me out. Their motto, All for One and One for All, stumbled when it came to homework, money, girls—just about everything that made a difference. Generally, it was more like, All control *in* one, and one controls all! You could see the tension in the control dynamic of the gang; whenever alcohol or weed or blunts were around, tensions rose between LeMarcus and Zorro. Bay Brother would doze out, Parrot would act silly, and yours truly would split. Sometimes, you could see that tension sizzle and pop on the checkerboard. When I awoke, Master Afri was carving away at his new project and dust flew.

You look sleepy brother Urchin. The coffee percolates, the bagels brown brother; time to rise and shine! Did you sleep well? asked my Master. Oh yes —great. *If the truth be told, every bone and muscle in my thighs and arms ached like crazy.* I said, I had a weird dream or two, but I slept great. *Put us back in the bed, cried my bones—immediately!* Well go upstairs and take a shower, said Afri (he had advised me to call him that; the word Master made him think of an era long gone. Even Master Afri was not to his liking. In a moment of hideous imagination, I had shortened the whole business to Master-Free! And those syllables gave me some kicks and giggles). Okay, be down in a few. I trudged upstairs, jumped in the shower, and heard the felicitous BONG of M3 as I soaped and scrubbed. After showering and drying, I peered into Master Afri's bedroom, which occupied only a quarter of the upstairs. Now I realized that the tall windows and high ceiling had been achieved by venting three quarters of downstairs space to the ceiling. Master Afri's bedroom stood in a quartered attic. The open side of the building housed tall windows up to the roof; shuttering of windows occurred with thick drapes, and from those drapes came—dust!

Feel better? asked Afri. Yes, yes...much better, I answered, stepping from the last stair. Urchin, meet Fergus, Fergus this is my apprentice Urchin. Glad to meet you Urchin; what an interesting name, said Fergus stepping forward and shaking my hand. Afri tells me that you have been helpful around the studio. It's great to see him as the Maestro of

Memphis art; I can tell you that his piece at the exhibit was a real triumph. Afri tell you about me and him? Tell you about those great days at the old barnyard? He doesn't want to hear about that stuff Fergus, said Afri. And to tell you the truth, I had never thought about my Master being in school, high school, junior high, or even elementary. I couldn't picture him as a student, but then I guess he had to grow up somewhere. Yeppee, said Fergus, old high school buds. Turning to Afri, he said, I like your studio man, you did a nice job reworking the space. Just like you, classy and clean—except for all this dust; lots of wood, many straight lines. Look—let's go get somewhere close, get some grit. Marmalades— Outta luck there man, said Afri, they don't do breakfast. Let's go to The Arcade, right on the corner; they got breakfast. Urchin, you ready, I nodded in the affirmative, letting my eyes perform a quick safety check; I overheard Fergus say to Afri, Man she is really banging some heads on that Board of Directors. She brought in a mediator, took some seminars in Eisenhower and shit, trying to make sure that she made some good tactical moves to get them to say yes on that Folkways Wing deal. And whew, she has some awesome chops brother—you ever watch her walk. Afri laughed and said, Homes, some things never change. Let's go.

Chops, I thought, *never heard of that! Must be legs—walkin' and such.* Now I almost could have done without breakfast, seeing as how I was still groggy, even with the shower, but I kept my mouth shut. Urchin, you okay? Said Afri. Never better, I said, sounding a bit like Fergus. He looked at me and smiled. It's a problem all the arts are having Afri, said Fergus, shifting into high gear as we walked to The Arcade. The symphony, the theaters, galleries, museums, libraries—probably the ballet also, he added. Afri said, Well my partner here is helping me to diversify a bit; he makes quills, engineers cleanup, and plans to create wooden puppets—the kind that operate with strings. I think he has talent hidden in those aching bones of his. Fergus said, Thing is, classical musicians are doing all the things that jazzers used to do; playing on street corners, night clubs—flat out hustling for gigs. Tell the truth, jazz and classical musicians—at least the intelligent ones, used to love to hear each other play and gently taunt one another in playful humor, both in written scores and improvisation. A fraternal kind of musical satire. You almost can't hear live jazz in Memphis anymore —weird! Afri chimed in as we reached the doors of The Arcade, Yeah, it's like the whole world wants to put on ear phones and go digital—they can't stand the sight of each other. In Memphis, that ingrown digital solitude is aggravated by the subterranean hum of racial conflict. But you can go to church and pave your way to heaven, as long as your Jesus is the same color you are.

    I really enjoyed your arrangement of that Firebird Suite, said Afri, I apologize for not hearing you guys down at the Cannon Center—I'm sure you played the shit out of that score. Urchin here has never been to a symphony concert in the hall, which is a shame because the acoustics and ambiance are awesome. Fergus said, Best be believing that homes; I'll get y'all some tickets. But check this, I thought, said Afri, You were teaching at the University also. I am, said Fergus, and I have some decent students, mostly from Memphis at the undergrad level and from all over at the graduate level. Frankly, many of them don't like to practice, or think they are smart enough to *skip* practicing; it's a shame when they can't invoke the playful discipline it takes to practice in really creative ways; find the fun in it! I could share awesome stories. Urchin, you have got to be bored with all this shop talk, said Fergus. Actually, I was glad to be along, thrilled to listen to these guys going at it, and overjoyed with the smell of the biscuits, bacon and eggs; and that was exactly what I ordered when the waitress came around, placing tall glasses of water on the checkered tablecloths before us in the booth where we sat.

Afri said, Let me get this right now, after high school you went—. Fergus said, To State, Michigan State. My high school teacher at Interlochen, Sidney Forrest—knew Keith Stein really well. I met Mr. Stein at Interlochen and he secured a band scholarship for me to attend State. He was a wonderful man and was the first to introduce me to double-lip embouchure. That's how you form your lips around the mouthpiece and reed.

My head would bob downward every now and then, and both Afri and Fergus would look over at me and crack up, but I just couldn't help it, and found my chin on my hands, my eyes peering through the bottom of my glass of water, at elongated red and white squares, waiting for a snake of some sort to wobble or wriggle past on the other side. Their voices went in and out of perception as I swear I saw a knight, a princess or king snake by on the other side of that glass.

We had some great conductors at Interlochen: Harry Begian, Kenneth Snapp, George Wilson, Freddie Fennell, Robert Russell Bennett, and played some fabulous music. The first audition piece I saw at Interlochen was the Firebird Suite. It's such a wonderful piece—had to practice it like a mad-dawg. *I could feel his eyes on me and I perked up a tad and even more as I saw that princess hopping around on those square. I wondered if Ramona looked like that:chops.* I had been through Klose, Baermann, Rose, and tons of sight-reading, but that Firebird was a whole new dimension, said Fergus, and I'd won that competition with the Navy Band in D.C. *I wondered if I could take out that King, skipping two squares at a time, with my bamboo gun.* One of our Memphis Phil conductors was at Interlochen too, said Fergus, And turned out to be quite a fine conductor—Alan Balter. Did you ever see him conduct? asked Fergus. Oh yeah, I remember him from those Sunset Symphonies you did downtown on the banks of Big Muddy, said Afri. *And I thought, looking through that glass of water, Yeah and the water in old Big Muddy was never this clear and then being suddenly startled by the arrival of our food.* Then I went to the Navy

Band—Anthony Mitchell was the leader then. He was wonderful to me also and a very intuitive conductor. Very passionate about music, just like Mr. Falcone at Michigan State. The good folks at State were great practice models—Elsa Ludewig, now Verdehr and Falcone practiced like crazy. Elsa taught me for a year when Mr. Stein was on sabbatical. She raised the clarinet standards at State by several miles. Many of the clarinet players both at Interlochen and in the Navy Band went on to have terrific careers; Howard Klug, Dave Breeden, Balter, Dave Shifrin, Lorin Levee—I am very lucky to have known them, and mouthpiece maker Mike Lomax, Larry Guy, Jay East, John Coulehan, and Ed Walters. Fortunate for me, I was accepted in the D.C. Band. Upon graduation from State, I was quickly classified as I-A during the Vietnam Conflict, even though I had an assistantship at the Peabody Conservatory.

But enough about me, where did you find this Urchin fella—looks like he wants to go to sleep on us. Yeah, said Afri, we stayed up kinda late last night chasing visions. Urchin—he said noticing that I was becoming more alert; *food glorious food!* Urchin, you gonna make it? he said. I nodded and tried to lift myself up saying, Oh yeah. What about the orchestra? Afri said, turning to Fergus, Are they going to turn the corner, survival-wise I mean? I sure hope so, said Fergus. A lot of people have put their heart and soul into that orchestra. De Frank swept floors and hefted stands to keep that orchestra rolling, Balter got the education piece right and had the orchestra rolling right next to the Mississippi. I wonder a little about some of the more recent hires made for the podium piece, though the musicians loved Jim Feddick. The community has to step up too—the musicians are well trained and are trying to put kids through college on almost poverty wages. I cannot imagine Memphis without an orchestra; I mean Memphis is where symphonic classics and the blues meet—you would think that a great symphonic masterpiece would germinate from those conditions. Perhaps the board has become lethargic. The visionaries necessary to invite minorities into the cultural life of the city don't exist—or if they do, they don't push the wheel. Seems to me like smart cities support platforms for ideas. I haven't seen the political leadership at concerts for a very long time. The stories in Memphis will probably have soundtracks made in Poland, and the stories are here, even if there aren't brains enough to get local arms around them.

Ramona talks about that too, said Afri. She thinks the various arts institutions need to band together with more energy. Folks would never substitute digital football for the real thing, but they think it's okay in the arts. Digital opera—Oh don't get me started on that, said Fergus. My greatest love so far in the orchestra has been playing zitzprobes. Coffee had come with my breakfast and I was fully alert now and was stunned by the word zitzprobe. I listened with a surge of energy, *zitzprobe*. What on earth is that, popping zits? asked Afri. Well that is really a sitting rehearsal—a rehearsal in which we play the music—say of Strauss or Puccini—with the singers, answered Fergus. It is an unbelievably wonderful experience in Rosenkavalier or Ariadne auf Naxos, just the pure music of singers and instrumentalists. The zitzprobe is like being in heaven! I dream of zitzprobes in the round with interaction between the audience and the performers—now that would be an experience treasured by audience members for ages, said Fergus laughing. At this moment, I wished I had my quill because I wanted to research that word, look it up for myself; but I held my peace; *zitzprobe*.

I had finished my meal when Afri ordered one last round of coffee. This guy Fergus turned out to be a real talker, kind of a grandstander, but I had enjoyed his presence. Look, he said, Ramona mentioned that you were kinda in a funk about the review. She feels like you should go soft on yourself about that review. Myself, I never read reviews; academicians like those things 'cause they document your expertise—or so they think. But think about it, even a re-creator, someone like me who creates the sound in the moment, but not the notes on the page, has to grow, develop—change—in order to keep from being bored about his or her work. When you experiment, there are no guarantees; sometimes an experiment works, sometimes it doesn't. An experiment is a strategic guess hopefully supported by positive statistics. Occasionally an experiment fails, not that yours did. Sometimes they go against the grain, not sometimes—many times. Critics don't like experiments; experiments take them out of their comfort zone. Here's what I think: a review is successful if it encourages the community at large to see or hear an exhibit or performance and make personal judgments about whether or not they like the art, love the music. A review should urge folks to think, to make up their *own* minds about the piece or performance.

Yeah, I know, but it still did kinda get to me, especially after all the hard work Ramona did, just to get the wing built, said Afri. Here's what I think—this city's cultural institutions have failed the black community. The education system has been close to the toilet—and I might add that institutions of higher education have not mounted a reading website and clinic, both face-to-face and on-line—that attacks illiteracy, the symphony has never commissioned a piece by a composer of color, the art gallery is trying, note you with the help of mediation, the ballet has taken big steps, and Hattiloo is *leaping* forward. Slavery, Jim Crow—hey growing up in Memphis, there were black and white signs all over the place. Only one of my clarinet teachers—Anthony Gigliotti—had a book in his library authored by a black writer. Wanna know what the book was? White Man Listen, Richard Wright. Now, just as there are white racists, there are black ones too, and too many of our brothers and sisters reject classical art, and the wonderful lessons contained therein, and therefore reject their own humanity. Why? Because the lessons contained in any great art form are human ideas first and foremost. And, too many of our brothers and sisters *refuse* to become great learners, and consequently read poorly, as documented by the appalling literacy rate of this town.

Preaching to the choir bro, that is exactly why I chose to pare down the Stravinsky and do what I can to support Ramona's efforts. To help the good folk, brothers and sisters, massas and missus, of every rank, persuasion, and color to understand the connection, the umbilical cord, between folk tale and classical phenomenon—or blues and symphony—to the choir my man! Stravinsky, Bartok, even Messiaen —devoted their lives to creating masterworks out of the magma of their environments. And what did it cost? For Stravinsky, he was astute as a business person; for Bartok it cost him his health; for Messiaen, he was lucky enough to get recorded. All I'm saying is that your personal vision, your artistic vision is important and that you—whether or not yonder critic appreciates it, understands or supports it —you have the right and responsibility to speak your peace, *not p-i-e-c-e*, and create what you have envisioned.

I was fully alert now, having heard those two going at it, battling like heavyweights about ideas, visions, communities, and art with hearts full of passion. It is a conversation that I will never forget. My Master, in his anguish, had told me about the money; the five, the seven thousand offered for the painting. In my heart, in my soul, I said; *tell him about the money!—tell Fergus about the money!!* If I had been a smarter fellow, I would have taken out my quill, slapped my face into fully awake, put in my two cents, and written the conversation down verbatim.

As it was, I ordered another two biscuits (Afri was paying) and stuffed them into my pockets. The only thing I now wished for was a fluffy pillow. My state of consciousness had ebbed and flowed, and I imagined that one was right there, right in the restaurant and I wished I could let my head crash right onto the table. When I felt this almost about to happen, both Afri and Fergus caught me by the arms and escorted me back to the studio. Upon arrival at the studio, a thousand BONGS of M3 would have found me inert.

VIII

My Master—well, he continued to make clear that this word master meant different things to different people—did not conceive of this word as signifying a master/slave relationship. To him, it was in no way similar to the connotation of one person giving orders and another taking orders. For him, and he stressed this numerous times, it meant one who was masterly, one who was on a journey to perfect his vision and had worked to master *skills* necessary to perfect that vision (in a democracy you *cannot* master people; the curious relationship he had with the euphemism *contraband* is significant in this quote; *only racists master contraband, he said, refugee is more appropriate*). As his apprentice, I was one who was just embarking on mastering those skills and would learn the craft of making art; this meant reading, researching, and skill improvement under his tutelage. In all honesty, I knew that his definition was the one that applied to me, one that needed me to be alert, quick, and responsive during my early stage. But my arms, back, and thighs told me that as well as being alert with my mind, I had to be strong of emotional stamina and physical endurance. Additionally, there were visitors who wanted to photograph the studio, townspeople who wanted autographs, phone calls that had to be answered, and congratulatory notes that had to be typed (he signed those). One of my responsibilities was just to be generally useful. In that regard, I had to separate the wheat from the chaff. These bits of minutiae, far from helping me to learn the grammar of craft, were time-consuming and could become monotonous. The sweeping, dusting, cleaning, fetching, hefting, and being useful started to impinge upon my time. There were indeed moments when I felt I was indeed a slave of the past; there were no whips and stakes, but occasionally my frustrations got the better of me and I would think, *do it yourself!* Thankfully, those moments were few and far between as Afri would intuit those moments when I came to my wits end and say, Urchin, it's time for you to get some real work done. I came to love that phrase real work and would rush over to M3 and celebrate with a BONG, and say, Real work time!

      To tell the truth, this folktale that seemed at once charming and haunting invaded my thoughts and infected my creative thinking, just like that snake had invaded my dream, just as the folk characters —the king and princess—sneaked up on me during breakfast and rolled behind my glass of water, trolloping across the red and white checkerboard table cloth. Was this an omen of some sort, a sign that my meager gifts were being wasted as a mere apprentice indentured to a mere mortal, hoping to replace a king? Could there be another answer? Perhaps my master had plans to publish his own critique of the critic in retribution for the lousy, stinking review? These questions sorted themselves out when I embarked upon a plan to find the real meaning behind this famed folktale. The movie of characters waltzing behind my glass of water in joyful frolic served to convince me that I had errantly chosen the wrong dialectic, chosen the paradigm of master in a kingly way, apprentice in a slavish sense. The solution to understanding this folktale would rest in my ability to flip the switch, turn the tables, trick the system, make master the slave and slave the master...the slave as king or even critic. The solution that I had hit upon centered on two sentences, formulated as I completed my daily chores and started doing my routine of drawing and copies using both my left and right hands. Here are the two sentences I came up with:

> When the Critic is presented with the feather (MemNoire) he demands the entire firebird or the death of the artist. The artist weeps back to his horse who instructs him to put corn (coin) on the fields in order to capture the firebird.

Obviously, the critic had coin to purchase MemNoire; I had not considered that a work of art could fetch that kind of money, capture that kind of attention. My master put his faith in corn, but not me! I knew the value of coin, and though young, I felt it my responsibility to mention this at a time early and convenient. It was then when I fully realized the animated gift that had been brought to me during that breakfast with Afri and Fergus. And it had all been animated by smoky snakes and shuffles of tales in glassed waters—would wonders never cease! The Critic was really after the princess and Afri's MemNoire was a ruse, a mere starting point for more luscious fare. I made up my mind to pursue this line of thought.

Phone calls continued to pester our, I mean my Master's studio, dust still wandered around alighting at its pleasure, and the carvings of wood multiplied and mushroomed into small statues made of clay, wood, plaster and—of all things—coat hangers. A BONG of M3 (in my absence, my master had attached the robust church bell to a rope, and the rope to the front door. In short, opening the door caused M3 to bellow!) rang into our sun-bridled space. Smack-dab before me, in short stacked heels controlled by a sprightly jaunt, a polka dot dress, neatly enclosed by a broad dark belt, the loveliest smile enclosed in an oval face and long deep, gorgeous black tresses, I have seen in my short span on earth. Hi, you must be Urchin! she said. To me, it seemed like her pronunciation flowed into the resonance of M3 for a very long time, dancing around the studio in copious echoes. It seemed as though featherbells in that black and white photo joined in, pealing away like little M3s celebrating the arrival of a princess. Ramona! said Afri, What a pleasant surprise! Ramona had shaken my hand and I refused to desecrate that touch with the contamination of dust. Ramona said, Afri, I had to make a quick run to the train station and thought I would stop by—good morning! Thought I would drop in and see what you guys are up to and I have a gift for your Maestro Urchin; I heard *Maestro* Urchin and electricity ran up from my coccyx bone through my spine, ringing my cranium like M3 in minor bongs.

Here you go, I framed a picture of you with MemNoire and put the review—oh-oh—I see you already have one on the wall. Ramona caught sight of the review that had been used for target practice and she laughed saying, I see you have already put it to good use—so you can put this one over your desk by your laptop, as a spare.

Afri said, You know that guy never introduced himself as a critic—that Hargrove fella. He was most unnerving and really didn't—I know Afri, said Ramona, taking a seat and revealing a pair of robust, almost athletic legs—the legs Fergus called chops. It doesn't really matter. The gallery has been flooded with visitors and folks are inspired with your MemNoire, especially young people. They say they can almost hear that bell ringing, almost touch the vibrations. He was probably just jealous of all those pretty women flocking around to hear you talk about —process! She got a kick out of the word for some reason; I couldn't figure that one out. She spoke in a low voice, and from time to time it faded out of range. I did hear Afri say, I'll make you a cup of coffee—check out my apprentice and his work. I think he has talent, and with dedication and practice, he might become a fine artist. I had my back to them as they talked and could hear, almost feel the movement of her low-heeled pumps as she approached my table, peering over my back to examine my drawings. I think you are right Afri, he does show ability. Ramona added, Now Urchin, be diligent and loyal in your commitment to Afri and to yourself, and listen well to his instructions and suggestions. He has your best interests at heart.

I hoped that she could not hear the bass drum beating in my heart. It has taken much hard work for Afri to get to this point in his career, she said to me, And he has a bright future. Afri gave her the cup of coffee and she took several long-throated gulps before saying, well I must run! Here Afri, here's a book on John Ward and an application form; both are yours. Take a look at this form first; I want you to complete this proposal for the gallery—it's a good chunk of money and involves a commission. I want you to apply for this—given the reaction to your painting, you are a shoe-in to win the commission. I'll expect to hear from you tomorrow. Come by early to my office. Thanks for the coffee and enjoy the framed photo, even if you can't stand the review! Master Afri's eyes trailed her as she left, and he said, Well Urchin—do you think she has chops? He chuckled, and then waved. The wave caused me pause—had she expected him to be watching her? Was she the target or was he the target? In which person would I find the golden goose?

She is lovely isn't she, said Maestro Afri. All in a few days I had made him Maestro, Master, King and Slave; he couldn't be as tired or confused as I was at this moment, and the golden goose part was still fresh in my mind. *Maybe what I need is a cup of coffee,* as I turned around, Master Afri handed me a cup, saying, Here's yours Urchin, I propose a toast to your apprenticeship. May your joys be healthy and everlasting. I said, Master Afri—why did you not tell her about the money? You haven't told her and you didn't tell Fergus either. I think that it is not right to cross things up like he did. He, that critic is really mad with you! Maybe jealous of the attention, but certainly really likes the work you created—since he offered you all that money for it! You might just be right Urchin—might be right. But for now, that's our secret, said Afri. Now Urchin we have a very big job to do and it will tax our abilities–both yours and mine. We do, I said quietly, How? We have a Firebird to catch and as soon as you are out of school, I'll need you here for eight-hour days. Talk to your Granny—I can talk to her if you like, and in the next few days tell me what you think. I include the version that prompted me in a new direction, both energetic and yet in many ways quite dangerous.

In this version a critic's artist is on a hunt and runs across a firebird's MemNoire. The artist's horse warns the artist not to touch it, as bad things will happen. The artist ignores the advice and seizes it to bring back to the critic so he will be praised and rewarded. When the critic is presented with the MemNoire he demands the entire firebird or the death of the artist. The artist weeps back to his horse who instructs him to put corn on the fields in order to capture the firebird. The firebird comes down to eat allowing the artist to capture the bird. When the critic is presented with the firebird he demands the artist fetch the Princess Vassilisa so the critic may marry her, otherwise the artist will be killed. The artist goes to the princess's lands and drugs her with wine to bring her back to the critic. The critic was

pleased and rewarded the artist, however when the
princess awoke and realized she was not
home she began to weep. If she was to be married she
wanted her wedding dress, which was under a rock in the
middle of the Blue Sea. Once again the artist wept to his
horse and fulfilled his duty to his critic and brought back
the dress. The princess was stubborn and refused
to marry the critic even with her dress until the artist was
dipped in boiling water. The artist begged to see his horse
before he was boiled and the horse put a spell on the artist
to protect him from the water. The artist came out more
handsome than anyone had ever seen. The critic
saw this and jumped in as well but was instead boiled
alive. The artist was chosen to be critic and married the
princess and they lived
happily.

    Maybe the princess was the problem; the king wanted the princess, but the princess hated the artist, not the king. This realization perplexed me for a few days as I went back, re-reading the folktale, spinning it out as I inhaled the dust of plaster and wood, the scents of paint and sawdust, as I cleaned and scrubbed the studio to free it of filth. I think these moments of drudgery, of moving—no, of shifting into a state of mental infatuation with the folktale—even as I performed physical labor, were amongst my fondest memories of my days as an apprentice. Master Afri knew I couldn't pay for my lessons. In reality, I was a student-apprentice gradually becoming infected with the joy of putting myself inside a folktale, with a movie animated by smoky snakes and shuffles of tales behind glassed waters. I was wading in the waters! Oh my, to my astonishment I started humming and singing that tune; Wade in the Water! I realized that I was chosen by my master to assist and learn. If the princess were the problem, then I should imagine her as the thief of the feather; and being a thief, she might desire the crown. In that way she could posses the crown of the king and scream orders, even to the poor horse. Certainly she desired the artist to be dipped in boiling water. The movie pursued me for many days and nights, though at night—my tired mouth being shut tight for obvious reasons—I was muted in my recollections of Wade in the Water. As I had never visited the gallery before, I accompanied my master there a few days later as he dropped off some papers; while I waited, I studied the various paintings and sculptures, examined the architecture of the place, and was hypnotized by a tall grandfather clock, encased in mahogany. Waving inside its interior was a long, golden second hand and a flipping hourglass of sand. Another thing I vaguely remember is the quizzical look my master shot my way when he heard me singing Wade in the Water out loud. Once he even joined me in singing that portentous tune in unison, banging old M3 in the rhythms and pulse of the rowing of an old slave ship. Whew, those were the days when the mind imagined freely and the muscles ached.

IX

The Board of Directors of the Brinks Gallery reflected the same perceptions and philosophies that lurked about the café tables and dining rooms of Memphis. Each of the assorted cultural institutions that populated the Memphis metropolitan area contained individuals who asserted themselves as experts—be it in education, music, art, drama, museums, religion or galleries. As a result, elected officials and public councils designed to lead citizens in a democratic meritocracy found themselves instead lead by self-proclaimed egotists ensnared in political battles, ruled by expert power technocrats wielding Robert's Rules of Order, and hog-tied by tacticians reigning with gigantic egos super-charged by personal fiefdoms.

Ramona Giovanelli had been fortunate in her recruitment of members for the Brinks Gallery's Board of Directors; among that board included Medis Steinbeck, one of the city's most outstanding attorneys in mediation resolution. Occasionally, the board suspended the procedures and methods of Robert's Rules, and meetings were led by Attorney Steinbeck in rounds which followed time-period constraints: free discussion (usually emotionally charged), one minute summaries to include one constructive suggestions (verbal and written) by each board member, plotting of pros and cons on a blackboard, and secret balloting after each discussion round. When meetings were led by Attorney

Steinbeck, Ramona would listen to the discussion and take notes, refusing to reveal her personal opinion on a given subject, and thanking members for their revelations. In that way, board members had been able to resolve sticky issues and minimize individual attachments to progressive or conservative ideologies that infected the discussions of teams designated to work for the good of the community. Two things now stood in her favor; one, she had won approval for the new Folkways Community Wing and two, she had negotiated a Director's Choice Award, to be given solely by her office. These methods were securely in place as Attorney Steinbeck moderated the usually fiery monthly board meeting following the popular success of the Petite Masked Ball.

We are not a damn charity, thundered Cameron Colfax, CEO of Service Unlimited, local business providing temps and laborers to shorthanded businesses in the metro area, we have the economics to consider...ticket prices are not covering our costs and attendance is down due to the recession. Our losses at the ticket window offset any gain in securing grants and parking concessions from city government—that's a zero sum gain. Our holdings and operating expense are average for our size—but we have little wiggle room to operate as we have in the past and must be vigilant in keeping expenditures under control. I hate to be a naysayer but even with the upswing in numbers due to the Masked Ball—there is a segment of the community that will not—or has not—supported the gallery over the long term. Should we continue on this path, a downturn in the economy could render our consequences catastrophic!

That's pejorative and unsubstantiated, shouted Julius Cooke from a seated position, You are evaluating a long-term program only recently put in place. This is an investment as much as a stewardship! This ballyhoo about balanced budgets is crazy; no one would borrow money if they were sentenced to a balanced budget on an hourly basis. Seems to me that's another ploy to short-shrift the outreach necessary to grow this enterprise. The philosophy we adopted to underscore this outreach is one which combines dedication through enhanced development—pdfs, video closeups, emphasis on education, community fellowship, and literacy—and engagement of artists with the community in partnerships. We've barely—look, the balance sheet formulates the arc of our targets and is well within our reach; the planning we have done keeps us within our budget for the fiscal year. With the shifts in emphasis we've made, ticket sales and streamlining in acquisitions, we stand to be closer to our budgetary targets than last year. Across the country, numbers are bad and Memphians understand the plight that we are in, the uphill battle that museums face, but we are righting the ship.

Colfax grunted, Uh-huh, well this capital improvement with the new wing and all should serve as a reminder that we must mind the perilous cliff on which we perch. You can call me whatever you like, but the money has to come from somewhere. What if these grants don't materialize? What if these on-line campaigns don't work? Look at the orchestra down the street—wonderful musicians damn near on the street! And I know the skinny on comfort zones! I will not trade my financial comfort zone hoping and praying that others, be they blue, green, black or yellow, will test *their* comfort zones and start to attend our exhibits. We have precious little wiggle room to operate people, we must be vigilant in keeping expenditures under control, comfort or no comfort zone!

Under control...there is the nub in its entirety, said Missy Shepherd, the sole African American on the board. You finally said the operative word. Take a walk through the gallery and note all that open space that *used* to be there is gone now! In a community that is 64 percent African American, we have an art gallery with little contemporary art and hugging zero from local artists. Why should the African-American public support an institution that refuses to reflect the creative accomplishments of members of their culture? Why should they have a European aesthetic shoved down their throat, when art enterprise of all ethnicities has been accomplished in sculpture, painting, and ceramics? That argument is ridiculous on its face and, I might add, that type of cultural dictation seems to take place across the board in the arts institutions of Memphis. The attitude promotes the very kind of racism that we are pledged to dilute and diversify—Look, we all, stuttered Cameron—I'm not finished! said Missy. Look at sports, football, baseball, basketball if you need lessons in commercialism; the sports drawing the greatest crowds have diversified—folks attend those events because they are diverse and therefore exhibit an unassailable meritocracy. Hell, everybody knows that societies of the past have favored friends, lovers, family members. Ain't no news there! The real question is will our blue-haired ladies and moneyed elite relinquish their choke-hold on the European axis elemental in this enterprise. The people, our recent admirers, see a new axis; they want to see meritocracy in action, democracy rising. Examine your mission and support the mission.

Well, I've listened to black music, said Tom Farley. Fact of the matter is there are some parts of black music that I love—but seems to me that most of it keeps the drums humming at fever pitch, and would not be appropriate to the concert hall and of course, we had some of that Rap stuff the other night, but right now we aren't the symphony. We certainly amplified our definition of the status quo then. Ahem, but we should remind ourselves that, historically, our black brothers and sisters have never consistently supported this gallery. I suspect their newfound attention might be short-lived.

There you go with that black crap once again Tom. A black composer won the Pulitzer just a few years ago, for your information, cried Missy. They haven't played that yet! I listen to guitars in country music and enjoy the stories; but we're talking about high art, art with no words in it! and selling tickets for that. You and I have had this conversation, heard this conversation all over Memphis. Our fair city sports a new spectrum of ethnicities for some time now. There might be more than a few golden geese in high-art, classical art, among them. Seems to me Ramona has got us pointed in the right direction.

Let me remind you folks, said Attorney Steinbeck, that the Director's job is to augment attendance, sustain our antiquities, and balance the bottom line of our operation. Of course, our job is to support the mission of this institution; to enrich the lives of our diverse community, expand our collection and varied exhibitions, and present dynamic programs that reflect the art of world cultures from antiquity to the present. We have work to do, ladies and gentlemen, and a course to chart. Let me also remind you that our Petite Masked Ball was a stunning success! Even with a momentary shortfall – which does not exist—in our operational balance sheets, we are on a bit of a roll! And, we have yet to learn of the choice our director will make will regard to the Director's Choice Award.

The ticks and tocks of the second hand on the grandfather clock reverberated in the silence, its metronomic movement seized the next sand-flipped hour. It echoed oblivious to the raucous tensions between board members pitting vision against finance. Ramona, free of the personal responsibility tied to leading the meeting, sat on the sidelines taking notes on crucial aspects of the meeting. Uppermost in her mind was the hope that she could weave a positive path through the ideological minefield and accomplish a golden patchwork that would keep the museum on course, perhaps even intuit the rational quilt effected by Attorney Steinbeck. Her visits to various high schools in the Memphis area convinced her that a wealth of artistic talent resided in the secondary schools. As a student in her hometown of Wash., D.C., she had grown up at the feet of the Freer, National, Corcoran, and Phillips art galleries. *How can we sit here at the top of this Delta crescent, and not have a wealth of vivid representations from African Americans of their life experiences; makes no sense?* Ramona's thoughts tumbled past the faces of Board members, and leapfrogged through Chicago, Detroit, and D.C.; *We have a wonderful opportunity to capture these ghosts and vibrations of a century of racial emotions and perceptions on canvas—now! I don't mean to miss it!*

Much of the music had found its way out of the Delta and photography had captured pictures from Jim Crow and segregation; but the therapeutic and artistic component had yet to be trapped, tamed, and vented in formal art. She had recently read an interview by Renzo Piano, architect, speaking of his work:

> The city is under your skin—as an Italian you grow up with this idea that cities are places where buildings talk to each other. There's a dialogue between the building

(painting) and the street. It's about accessibility, it's about civic life. An urban person is a person that knows how to behave with civility, how to share, how to be accessible. A building (painting) should be like that. It should talk to the city, talk to the people. Buildings (paintings) like this allow people to share experiences together, to enjoy and share life. Speaking together is a form of acceptance and the beginning of tolerance, which is the secret of civic life.

That's where I am headed, she thought smiling to herself, to nurture the secret of civic life right here in good old Memphis. She watched the meeting with great interest, carefully noting the energy with which the issues facing the gallery were being contested and debated. In the end-of-round one-minute summaries, normally quiet members of the board spoke with great enthusiasm about the momentum and positive comments they had received from community members. Hargrove, invited as a non-speaking observer, sat silently petrified by the frank and honest tilling of racial soil, watching roots and tributaries, mouth agape.

Erma Nightingale stood quietly in the back, cleared her throat, and said, I promise to get right to the point here. As I said last time in my comments on the new wing, the African Diaspora is seriously under-represented in this gallery; anybody that thinks otherwise is just plain stupid. Fact of the matter is, we have a ton of free space here and need to attract people, attract the community, to the premises. For health reasons, I have not been as diligent as I would like regarding our latest numbers, our accounting. For my tastes, our collection is on the smallish side. Still we are trying to remain true to our mission, hoist the flag of art high, have the citizens of Memphis haul ass over here to witness some of the great antiquities of the West and hope they have a civilizing effect on our Memphis brethren, demonstrate the artistic possibilities in democratic culture, commission some pieces here and there. Bravo to our directress. As one who regularly ventures into Memphis spaces and loves the arts, I think we can all be very proud of the efforts we are making to re-create our community. Certainly her efforts have been most remarkable and the Petite Masked Ball was one of the most racially diverse I have seen in this town in recent years. I can guarantee that this effort will pay off, both in this gallery and the community at large. Therefore, my suggestion would be to let the wind fill the sail, step up requests for donations—especially through emails and on-line—and invite your friends and relatives to come out to check out our exhibits.

Steinbeck had navigated the brittle and raw commentary with the aplomb of a tightrope walker, consummately felicitous, wondrously feline and diplomatic. Now, we have heard from all of you and I have your written commentary regarding issues raised in tonight's meeting, she said. Let me tell you that I admire the energy and frankness with which you have shared your thoughts and feelings. We are going to strap this boot tonight and use it to kick our efforts into high gear; we have everything we need to weave boot-strings through hooks up from the ankles, bring the sides together, and drop-kick our mission way down the road of success! Steinbeck circled the pros and cons, yanked the sides together, gave a brief exposition on the path of resolution, and took cellphone photos of the result. If you have written comments, write those down and send them to us. This meeting is adjourned.

Once free from after-meeting quarterbacks, Ramona made a beeline for her office. She took a deep breath and laid her notes on her desk, satisfied that the meeting had resolved in sound strategy to support the new wing and keep in place the next step, the Director's Choice Award. Director Giovanelli reached into her purse for a match, lit a Virginia Slim, and watched the smoke billow into free space. Good, that is a relief, she thought taking a seat behind her desk, and that Hargrove kept his sermons to himself. *Working to demonstrate a strong connection between folk and classical art seems like even a better move now than it was a few days ago. And they left the grants office alone, thank goodness. Plus, no doublespeak about the Pacific Rim and its business opportunities, though we've got to make sure that we do some research into securing additional Oriental and Hispanic art.* She glanced at the clock which read 11:25 pm. As she took a final drag and doused the smoke, a knock came on the door.

X

Must be George checking up on me before he leaves, we are lucky to have a janitor as conscientious—. She opened the door and said, Hargrove—I thought everyone had left! I'm so glad you were able to attend the meeting tonight! Won't you—Hargrove had already stepped by her and stood in front of her desk, craning backwards at her with a wide grin. Such a fine meeting and you didn't even have to engage personally in a battle of wits, he said, I am more impressed with your administrative wizardry each time I witness you in action. Scrutinizing her desk in mere seconds, he took note of the folktale printed on the program of the Masked Ball. As it was upside down he could not read it, but he *could* make out the name Afri Walker on the manila folder—though it was upside down as well. Congratulations! he said.

My, my Hargrove, you are kind. What can I do for you? I was just tidying things up before locking my office—you must have something on your mind—you were so quiet tonight and we always cherish our cultural critic; you have so much to add to our discussions; *jackass, and you obviously have some bit of minutiae you want to lobby me about.* Ramona you give me much too much credit. I merely noticed your light on and thought I might share a word or two. Obviously, the board has great faith in you, as do I, and glories in these recent successes you've navigated in the community. She stood in her stocking feet, having kicked off her shoes and registered surprised knowing that she yet stood a few inches above Hargrove without the elevation of short heels. Well, continued Hargrove, so much of my recent email has referenced the review I submitted to my editor about the Petite Masked Ball—such a stellar event. I never suspected so many of our fellow citizens were following the gallery with such interest. Unfortunately, quite a few readers felt that I unfairly singled out MemNoire, that evocative cherub by Afri Walker, felt I singled it out in my review, unfairly evaluated his MemNoire and hardly mentioned the other pieces in the exhibit. Indeed, Hargrove, said Ramona, I noticed that there was scant mention of the other nine pieces. My take on that, said Ramona taking a seat behind her desk, Perhaps there is some other truth in it, perhaps you have a bit of distaste, not so much with the artist, as with abstract expressionism—or vice versa—? How do you assess developments?

Exactly the case, though probably there is more than my predilection for naturalistic—er, *tonal*—pieces, said Hargrove adding, And my editors at the newspaper cut out my commentary about the other nine for idiotic reasons having to do with space constraints that I knew nothing—I didn't know you smoked! *And you would never smoke out my strategic thoughts about whatever, you old goat.* Ramona said, Did you ask them about—enjoin them to print the balance—Oh they would never do that, said Hargrove, They just carry on careening this way and that, making odd decisions—unfathomable ones. Anyway, I just stopped by to—Hargrove, said Ramona, I think you should encourage the paper—your editor, to print the balance of your review. Just the mention of the other artists would help us immensely and support our good will with them, get them in front of the general public! I mean, usually—*she felt herself moving into high gear now*—you balance things out...strengths and weaknesses, encourage attendance and self-made opinions, event times, maybe some pictures here and there sprinkled with your personal opinions. But we always count on you to nudge the public to get out, see for themselves, and arrive at their own opinions. So, perhaps the clientèle—*ah, that word felt so good leaving my throat, remind him that he too has a business interest in all of this*—your clientèle, she said, of the Commercial Flyer—has much at stake where the arts are concerned; *wonder how his tastes run in classical music—does he like high dissonance Schoenberg, murmuring Bartok—meditative Messiaen, boisterous Stravinsky?* And you didn't mention our puppet show; we got rave feedback on that!

By the way, how did you like the Firebird Suite performed by the orchestra recently, she said trying to get a fix on his tastes in contemporary classical music, You know of course that Fergus—the clarinetist—plays with them regularly. Oh yes, piped Hargrove, I understand that they played unusually well, unfortunately I missed that concert with a bout of that bug—or whatever it is that's going around. But I did get a chance to chat with Mr. Walker—about his

MemNoire, and note with interest that his background includes study abroad. I do think that elevates him to a unique status...such an unusual name for a painting...felt it my responsibility to single him out—for special attention. Somewhat negative! said Ramona anticipating his direction adding, He is quite a fine artist and is gaining reputation nationally. In my opinion, his work is unusually fine. He wants to keep MemNoire in Memphis—keep it here at the gallery to inspire our public. In fact, he has given us first option on its purchase, should we choose to go down that road! Hargrove said, Offered the gallery first option? I thought—Ramona blurted, You thought what, Har—the moment caught her by surprise, as did the path of the conversation, as did her tone of voice, and somewhere deep down, she intuited—realized that money had been discussed with Afri regarding the work. *You made him an offer...and did he refuse? accept?—tell you the piece was not for sale; you jackas*s! Now Har-grove, she said in poised recoup, tracking his temperament, tuning the music of his name, I have to tell you that we don't want the black community to mutiny on us as it seems they have with the orchestra. Look around, look at the movies, the plays, the wealth of Jim Crow and Civil War stories in our Southern midst, TV, sports—diversity is big business! And in the South things are changing as never before. Blacks are spending their entertainment dollars to see if meritocracy works, to see if democracy works, to see if European education stretches, to test classical music and experiment with how to change it, how to put *their* stamp of approval on it. And believe me the classics will change, just as the arts are changing. Help us to change it Hargrove —*oh god, my mouth has been over-shut too long in that meeting. Forgive my trite sermon*—My fault, said Hargrove making awkward, sudden steps toward the door, I suspect that I've kept you up far beyond your bedtime. Goodnight, and he fairly trotted towards the foyer.

Ramona watched as Hargrove disappeared in to the shadows and darkness of night, and took long deep breaths as she clicked off her office lights and stepped back inside, shutting the door. The picture window of her office overlooked Overton Park and she allowed the carpet of city lights, shadows and velvet blacks coming through abundant, majestic trees to wash over and through her. She teased herself with phrases, jazzy counterpoints to those taunt folktale phrases; the firebird sculpts the sculptor, the sculptor fetched his masterwork under a rock, if she was to be married she wanted M3, the feather wanted its firebird, the queen was dipped in boiling water. Moonbeams lingered across her desk, and Ramona opened the windows to let in fresh air; *I didn't know you smoked?* massaged edges of her memory. How about the sculptor under a rock? her lips asked her, pouting comically in the reflection of office glass. She would not use the gallery to promote mere consumerism, but the path to the environment of learning she sought might need to travel through consumer territory; *tools of capitalism, and everyone gets a chance to be dipped in boiling water. She sat behind her desk, bent to put on her shoes, finger-flexed the folktale, held it awash in luminous moonbeams. The king begged to see his feather before he was boiled.* The thought tickled her and in that moment, she penned the following version of the folktale:

In this version a director's archère is on a hunt and runs across a firebird's feather. The archère's horse warns the archère not to touch it, as bad things will happen. The archère ignores the advice and takes it to bring back to the director so she will be praised and rewarded. When the director is presented with the feather she demands the entire firebird or the death of the archère. The archère weeps back to her horse who instructs her to put corn on the fields in order to capture the firebird. The firebird comes down to eat allowing the archère to capture the bird. When the director is presented with the firebird she demands the archère fetch the Prince Vassiliant so the director may marry her, otherwise the archère will be killed. The archère goes to the prince's lands and drugs him with a wine to bring him back to the director. The director was pleased and rewarded the archère, however when the prince awoke and realized he was not home he began to weep. If he was to be married he wanted his masterpiece, which was under a rock in the middle of the Blue Sea. Once again the archère wept to her horse and fulfilled her duty to her director and brought back the masterpiece. The prince was stubborn and refused to marry the director even with his masterpiece until the archère was dipped in boiling water. The archère begged to see her horse before she was boiled and the horse put a spell on the archère to protect her from the water. The archère came out more beautiful than anyone had ever seen. The director saw this and jumped in as well but was instead boiled alive. The archère was chosen to be director and married the prince and they lived happily.

From somewhere out of the deep blue sea came a lovely memory:

> *Hi princess! Hi Daddy—Daddy did you have a good day? Of course princess—a wonderful day and now you just made it better! Tell me about your day, Daddy. Well Daddy met with some students and then he practiced for a concert...and the practice session went great. Now you tell me about your day, princess. Okay, well I drew pictures of Mommy and flowers. Then we played dodgeball, jumped rope, and blew bubbles. Daddy you forgot! I did? Yes Daddy, you promised to take me to the park when you got home—can we go now, just for a few minutes, please, please? Right now? Uh-Huh! Well I need to go give Mommy a kiss, can you wait a minute? Okay—but just one kiss Daddy, not two. As they walked across the Hampton Institute campus, the hourly sound of church bells blossomed all around them. Why do those church bells ring Daddy? They ring to remind us of the people we love; of our ancestors gone before, cherie!*

The second cigarette was the only thing she carried with her from the building besides her purse. She lit it once seated in her car; the fired, bright tip of hot tobacco crackled as she inhaled and as she exhaled through the smoky haze of ringlets, she witnessed the dark night, sparkling with car lights and neon signs in motion and reaching her through the haze of her car cabin's clouds. Graffiti from the other side of Poplar avenue provided a canvas for the din; murals and music—form a street partnership with the symphony. *What to call it?* Call it Murals and Music—we can do that anywhere! You were right Hargrove—you sure didn't know that I smoked—I sure am smoking right now! *Oh yeah—Murals and Music.*

XI

Before I knew it, the last days of May were approaching, and I stood facing the possibility of day-long summer employment. The king's crown which I had painted in black and white still graced the concrete wall across the street from the studio, but it had morphed into a more cloud-like form, changed into a shape less angular, more rounded and iridescent! I shrugged off a close look attributing its puffiness to weathering. Could its fluffiness, enhanced by facing eastward and bleached by spears of radiant sunlight, result from natural causes? After all, who cares about graffiti blistered into blemished round edges; *it ain't no mural!* Anyway, the day held promise of beauty; soon after I dusted the studio, M3 announced Fergus with a BONG!

I just love that sound, said Fergus skipping over to touch vibrating M3, and with glee he added, Top of the mornin'! And M3 sang echoing each word —*ong, ong, ong*! Brother Fergus, said Afri, You showed up! Brother Afri my *maaiiin* man, said Fergus, If I said I was coming brother, it's going to happen! Wanted to get that bird's eye, close up view of your studio that I missed the last time. By the way Urchin, here's a feather I found outside my apartment. Thought that such a distinguished enterprise as yours could use another bit of pluck! and he handed me a large crow's feather. I noticed that in his other hand he held a briefcase and Afri asked, Did you bring your clarinets? Oh yeah, said Fergus, gonna serenade you guys a bit, show good Urchin here what he's been missing analog style—say, I missed these two faces on your church bell the last time. Looks like Malcom X on one side—And Martin on the other, said Afri. Now that's kinda deep, said Fergus, almost like a goalpost, and the *bong* celebrates the two of them. You got it, said Afri, for young boy here as a gentle *sound* reminder—both those guys got killed, one a man of peace, the other a militant brother, a man of by-any means-necessary—and though their methods were different, for a person of color there are major challenges to carve a life of meaning in this country as it currently stands. Now there's a lot of message in that! said Fergus, I knew I would pick up some tips about mastery! Bongs through goal posts—!

So good bro tell me about you, said Afri, I've been reading about the orchestra and its troubles. Understand that you folks are having to make more serious cuts in your budget, losing some musicians and taking hits in your salaries. What's up with all that? I remember y'all from the days of that clarinetist-conductor in the white suit, right down on the river and old Jimmy Hyter singing those never ending renditions of Old Man River! Things took a turn for the worse, didn't they?

Fergus stepped to the washbasin, rinsed his hands, started unpacking his clarinet, and stuck a reed in his mouth. Yeppee, he said talking through the side of his mouth, Hyter had a real good time with all that.

And the town was going crazy with thousands down on the river screamin' and hollerin' for more Tote that barge—lift that bale!

Dead right—Tote that bale—b-a-i-l! And they both laughed. You can't imagine what a thrill it has been for me to be in the orchestra through the thick and thin of it. And you know from when I was in high school...you were a few years after me, but ever since being a kid, I have loved the sound of music ensembles—to play in the middle of that orchestra over the years has been a great treat; always said to folk that I had the best seat in the house. I have *Vincent DeFrank* to thank for that opportunity! Bail us out my brother! This is a clarinet reed Urchin, he said, In order for the clarinet to make a sound, this reed has to vibrate. Afri said, So do you think the orchestra will recover? I mean...what do you think caused the problem? Well, said Fergus, there is a lot of blame and finger pointing; from my perspective, there is enough blame to go all around. At one point, we felt like the town was ready to go into lift-off mode, go international. We played symphonic war horses, locked horns with both the gospel and country folks—talked about building a hall worthy of the music enterprises that have become the city's hallmark and attracted some fine musicians.

Yeah, and lately we hear very little about the orchestra, said Afri, and you have that wonderful new hall. It's almost like we are constantly bailing water out of a sinking ship. All around the country the scene seems to be the same—but—don't get me started. I could tell stories, said Fergus, and as communications between the musicians and the board became less candid, those two groups seemed to interact less and less—like a bad marriage, where you get to a point that you just even don't want to think about it, much less argue face to face. Parties get stuck in their postures and accusations fly in the spaces that love used to occupy. In the silence I thought, *Accusations fly in the spaces that love used to occupy;* that sounds like a title for a blues tune! Afri said, Well its been a while since I heard you guys in the Cannon Center—heard y'all when it first opened up; man the sound was amazing—and you could hear the softs and fortes, clear articulations and balances masterfully done. The sound is still there, said Fergus, the concept of undistorted beauty; but if something—he shook his head, pursed his lips—Hey all this doom and gloom.

Afri noted the silence saying, I got some coffee brewing big brother and some more shit brewing I need to tell you about. My boy here, Mr. Apprentice Urchin manifests a good artistic eye; he doesn't know it yet, but he going to be right here full-time in the summer—ain't that right Urchin—yeah, and his puppets—look at 'em—those puppets are first class! In that moment, I am sure that I felt more prideful than John Q. A. Ward, apprentice and student under sculptor Henry Kirke Brown. The silver keys of the clarinet sparkled as the sun outside rose skyward; *play something, play anything!* I sighed in silence, though my heart skipped a beat or two hearing those compliments about my puppets. Thought you would never ask, said Fergus, tooting on the mouthpiece, testing the sound of the instrument briefly. Let me drag out my clarinet score—Urchin, this is what my part, the part I made for the Masked Ball, looks like—and here is the master score, with all the parts on it for piano, violin and clarinet. He gestured for me to hold this part, which I did and said, Okay, here we go with a Rose etude. These etudes are studies designed to aid the clarinetist in his or her development, or as a gentle reminder of basic skills essential to achieving mastery in performing on the instrument. We have many gestures—abstract gestures without the instrument in hand—like coordinating fingers, raising and lowering fingers quickly or slowly, creating and supporting the wind column, and the formation of the embouchure; the gestures register real when we actually play the instrument. Afri brought Fergus some coffee—which our guest briefly sipped—and sat beside me to watch.

    Fergus' clarinet tones soared and sallied about the studio, his fingers caressing the keys in slow, careful movements, falling and rising in a velvet, singing line which shone in a golden voice, sparkling as if a sun behind a flock of clouds. If I were to pick a color, it would be one of resonant golden-orange dressed in deep purples in the low register. I imagined my crow's feather, a rich shroud of black velvet mounted upon those shimmering gleams and golden tufts of clouds. A feather without a bird, weaving and pivoting on my canvas of air, painting in veils of transparencies, veins, ellipses and arcs in similarity with all that abstract expressionism that my master loved to portray. But the sounds and patterns of the etude, the wind column of the clarinet nursing purplish tones in its low register and golden orange in the middle, snatched my feather from me, mounted it on each separate note, and tossed them about in the studio as a sonorous featherbed of sounds, ambling and dodging, trilling above and beyond the dust. Hey, said Fergus, snatching the clarinet from his mouth. I almost forgot a humorous gift I concocted for the Masked ball which I forgot to read to the audience; I brought it along and hope you like it; as we listened, he read the following ditty:

A Conductor's Clarinetist is on a hunt and runs across a firebird's feather. The Clarinetist's horse warns the Clarinetist not to touch it, as bad things will happen. The Clarinetist ignores the advice and takes it to bring back to the Conductor so he will be praised and rewarded. When the Conductor is presented with the feather he demands the entire firebird or the death of the Clarinetist. The Clarinetist weeps back to his horse who instructs him to put corn on the fields in order to capture the firebird. The firebird comes down to eat allowing the Clarinetist to capture the bird. When the Conductor is presented with the firebird he demands the Clarinetist fetch the Orchestra so the Conductor may marry her, otherwise the Clarinetist will be killed. The Clarinetist goes to the Orchestra's lands and drugs her with a wine to bring her back to the Conductor. The Conductor was pleased and rewarded the

Clarinetist, however when the Orchestra awoke and realized she was not home she began to weep. If she was to be married she wanted her masterpiece, which was under a rock in the middle of the Blue Sea. Once again the Clarinetist wept to his horse and fulfilled his duty to his Conductor and brought back the masterpiece. The Orchestra was stubborn and refused to marry the Conductor even with its masterpiece until the Clarinetist was dipped in boiling water. The Clarinetist begged to see his horse before he was boiled and the horse put a spell on the Clarinetist to protect him from the water. The Clarinetist came out more handsome than anyone had ever seen. The Conductor saw this and jumped in as well but was instead boiled alive. The Clarinetist was chosen to be Conductor and married the Orchestra and they lived happily.

I like the way that turned out, whaddaya think? said Fergus. We gave Fergus the Main Street version of a standing ovation. Master Afri said, Fergus, Urchin is unfamiliar with the journey held in your version, the journey of your clarinetist towards mastery, the desire of your orchestra towards its masterpiece. Fergus thought for a moment and said, This piece of African blackwood has inspired me on a very long journey. My first clarinet teacher, Sidney Forrest, made a wonderful recording of Weber's Grand Duo Concertante, which I heard as a ninth grader. Mom had signed me up for clarinet lessons with another fellow, but I heard this recording and harassed her to let me study with Mr. Forrest. He had been teaching at the National Music Camp, at Interlochen Michigan, and got me admitted there; that was a great experience with awe-inspiring conductors; Kenneth Snapp, Harry Begian, Robert Russell Bennett, Frederick Fennell—I loved playing for George Wilson, truly a remarkable man, with an incomparable beat pattern; both clear, precise and greatly nuanced. It's been a great journey towardsmastery—oh, and I remember the trip to Interlochen. There was this drunk Pullman's porter, a black man with an engineering degree in the forties, and as we talked about his inability to find a job, we pulled into Pittsburgh at night and the lights of the steel mills made it look like a starry night in the heavens; truly a magnificent sight!

I considered the orchestra in search of its masterpiece, the princess in search of the dress she embroidered, Las Siestas in search of reading talent, my good fortune in having the opportunity to develop my carving ability, realizing that they all were energized by a search for finding, realizing, developing the fruits of their talents, a curiosity for sustaining the tactical strategies necessary for my growth. *Do I have the character, energy, curiosity and discipline for this?* I asked myself, hoping that my journey, my energy would be likewise sustained. Fergus took another sip of coffee and said, Now I have my part for the Firebird arrangement and I want to share it with you; I'll start with the mournful song of princess Vassilisa and then play excerpts of the firebird fluttering about. I watched as his fingers skittered and skated about the keys. Man, those arpeggios were really wicked, said Afri when he finished. Oh yeah—lucky for me, I memorized those bad boys fairly early on. Many of our conductors liked to dance as you play that passage. Almost turn into a monkey on the stage. Dick Reynolds was the principal clarinetist when I started with the orchestra and he had been all over the world as a naval officer; he had a great sense of humor and shared wonderful stories. He'd studied with Victor Polatschek—that man loved the clarinet and knew the BSO clarinet section personally, had the clarinet section of the Met over to his house when the opera came to Memphis. And he told a full course meal of jokes; we had a great time in the orchestra. Of course Vincent De Frank was the conductor then, and he worked his fanny off establishing the symphony in Memphis. He built the library—which they had better audit—set up stands, worked with the school system establishing mini-concerts on Fridays. A ton of folks have worked extremely hard to nurture the orchestra. The Cannon Center is one of Memphis' great jewels, the Cannon Center and the Hooks Library. Alan lobbied hard for that building; he and the Cannon family and Martha Ellen got that done! Martha Ellen had an amazing gift for developing administrative talent. Since Balter, the orchestra has struggled a bit. Balter was a huge ham, loved to play and continued to play as a conductor; we were competitors at Interlochen. That tradition helped the musicians feel like the conductor wasn't merely a kingpin, a musical emperor, but that he or she still struggled towards mastery on an instrument, as a performer...Bernstein, Szell, or dabbling in Opera from either posture. Opera teaches the most obstinate conductor patience and plasticity. Conductors of the recent past have been emperor-smitten—we've had flailing arms in stove-piped suits bedeviling us with beat patterns impossible to follow, attitudes seemingly contemptuous of the musicians, and egos wishing to put podium-praise in our mouths. Some-body overheard a relative of one ego utter, Now the sonuvabitch wants to be a conductor! And many have the nerve to nurture mini-mafias within the ranks of the orchestra family.

  The orchestra desperately needs a caring lover of people and musicians, someone who wishes to seize a prime developmental opportunity. I felt that immediately when I engaged with superb colleagues at the university, Eaheart, Dolph, Lynch; each had a love for people and music. I cannot imagine a town that loves music more than Memphis that has experienced conductors with any poorer senses of rhythm! The town is ready: teaching cameos, video screens, conversations between board members and musicians, public polling for repertoire, and patron reviews—a ton of possibilities. And some commissions here and there; short and cheap at first. If transparency is needed, put the financial books on the net. We had Anton Copolla here for Opera Memphis; he is a wonderful conductor and personality; and a beat like Leinsdorf or Mehta! A few flags—colorful flags—for the Memphis Phil downtown, an air raid (*Batman, I thought*) light to announce concerts, free rent for the orchestra, and the beat would be on! My most memorable musical experience was a *zitzprobe—a sitting rehearsal with no staging, just the singers and orchestra exploring the opera score*—for Ariadne auf Naxos; that was like having the steel-factory lights of Pittsburgh and the sounds of heaven at your feet. Memphis has literacy issues—big time; the orchestra could be a big help with that. A little schmoozing from the political leadership and investigative journalism from the papers would help too, added Afri, and the brothers and sisters need to get off those wide booties! Amen brother Afri, said Fergus, skipping across the open space. I thoroughly enjoyed hearing them banter about that day; *what is it that my Master wants to tell him about?*

XII

Afri Walker rose early, checked his clock, rinsed his teeth, and showered hurriedly on the day after his visit with Fergus Baptiste. *Man, Fergus sounds good, played his ass off yesterday—great to see him. Forgot to fill him in on that application for the commission grant. Guess it's just as well; if it comes my way, I'll make sure that he hears about it.* Quiet reigned in the studio and he stepped to M3 and rang it by hand, soaking up the sound, letting his eyes scan the studio's untidy appearance, thinking about the next steps he wanted to take with his new idea.

In this version an Artist's Curiosity is on a hunt and runs across a Controversy's feather. Curiosity's horse warns Curiosity not to touch it, as bad things will happen. Curiosity ignores the advice and takes it to bring back to the Artist he will be praised and rewarded. When the Artist is presented with the feather he demands the entire Controversy or the death of Curiosity. Curiosity weeps back to his horse who instructs him to put corn on the fields in order to capture the Controversy. Controversy comes down to eat allowing Curiosity to capture the bird. When the Artist is presented with the Controversy he demands Curiosity fetch Creativity so the Artist may marry it, otherwise Curiosity will be killed. Curiosity goes to Creativity's lands and drugs her with a wine to bring her back to the Artist. The Artist was pleased and rewarded Curiosity however when Creativity awoke and realized she was not home she began to weep. If she was to be married she wanted her Muse, which was under a rock in the middle of the Blue Sea. Once again Curiosity wept to his horse and fulfilled his duty to his Artist and brought back the Muse. Curiosity was stubborn and refused to marry the Artist even with her Muse until Curiosity was dipped in boiling water. Curiosity begged to see his horse before he was boiled and the horse put a spell on Curiosity to protect him from the water. Curiosity came out more handsome than anyone had ever seen. The Artist saw this and jumped in as well but was instead boiled alive. Curiosity was chosen to be Artist and married Creativity and they lived happily.

Afri ran his fingers along the oblong hulk of plaster he had dried overnight on extra palettes and placed center most in the studio. Things were becoming a little cramped in the studio and he reflected on the application, the visit, Ramona as a possible model for his apprentice, and the drawings he'd made recently, for his new idea. It was a controversial idea, as was his idea for M3; *but if I cannot be controversial in art, then how can I inaugurate a fresh approach to the understanding of a new social wave, a higher evolution, a new level of meritocracy in the history of American society?* Next to his bed stood a copy of a book by Abraham Bolden —an account of his history as the first black in the President's Secret Service. The idea stalked him for some time after seeing the performance of Baptiste's Firebird arrangement; reflections on the folktale urged him to seize it as vision, one with renewed emphasis on the kinship between folk and classical art, between the popular and the intellectual, the commonplace and mythical, as a means of stating this in a plastic art, a means of realizing this rapport in sculpture. *I just can't believe that a city with the caliber of literacy issues alive in Memphis gets minimal support from its major university for the public schools—especially in reading, minimal support for integration in its churches, stodgy and contested support for that Folkways Wing from the Brinks—finally some progress with the Hooks Library and Hattiloo Theater. And Shelby County boasts the highest inheritance wealth in the state!*

A BONG announced the arrival of Urchin and he said, Hey Urchin, great to see you ! Look, I've got a ton of stuff I want to get started on. Here, let me show you the drawings I've done so far. I want to do a moderate-sized sculpture—that's why I had you clean out that area over there and help me build that sand pit. Also, I have some fellas coming over in the next coupla days to rebuild that furnace. I saw some drawings of a furnace that was built without a chimney right before the Civil War by a guy named Karl Richter. We are going to try that style of furnace; supposedly, it will be more efficient and allow me to achieve some of the effects I want in this new sculpture. I had some real problems with that bell...with M3...want to see if I can solve some of those problems. If I have success this time, then we are good to move on to some more projects in the same vein, if not...well, let's think positively. Okay, so this project will be a bird—inspired by your fascination with feathers and the folktale arranged by Fergus. One wing will sweep downward—and be fully represented—like this, and Afri held up his drawing for his apprentice, so the boy could see the effect he was after. It's a full representation of the wing, said Afri, embroidered by individual feathers—imitating the ones you have already drawn and the quills you have made—and the other wing arcing upwards towards the sky. That wing—the arcing one, will be transparent—see-through in a sense, and allow the viewer to see the sky and layers of the bird's body. On the side where the wing is natural, the viewer will see into the skull, as if looking at an x-ray. On the side where the head is natural, the body will have layers of sinew, muscle and skeleton.

I—said Afri—and a BONG whistled by from M3, as a delivery boy announced, Delivery for Maestro Afri Walker. I am he, said Afri. Please sign here sir, said the young man. Afri signed the confirmation as the boy said, Gosh, you're an artist! I sure wish I could draw—tried in high school, but— Not to give up, said Afri, there's always time—but you have to make time to learn anything! Got that mister, said the fellow, turning and BONGing on his way out. Urchin had a reasonably good idea of how the piece was to shape up, but he had not seen the process. Afri turned on the computer so that he could witness the drawings to be made on plaster while he would assist the bricklayers in their restructuring of the furnace. As Urchin studied the anatomy of the bird, he watched Afri open a slim box containing featherbells and a card. Jeez, said Afri, casting aside the green paper enveloping the gift, somebody sent flowers—hey there's a card! Heavens my man, we got us a commission, oh-wee! A commission for a sculpture lil' brother! Ooow! What? said Urchin, you —we have a commission—so what does that mean? said Urchin. It means, said Afri, that the Brinks Gallery and their Board of Directors has given us some money to work on a project, a sculpture that will reside on their premises, in their museum for public display! Afri showed the letter to Urchin with a proud whoop and gift of featherbells appeared to ring and tinkle right in the air. Afri said, This is great luck, great luck Urchin—it's almost as they if could read my mind! Urchin wondered what all this meant and was even more surprised when his master picked him up and whirled him around. He had been thinking about that oblong hunk of plaster that stood in the middle of the studio floor. For his part, Afri had been deep in thought about his young apprentice and a fear had risen in his thoughts.

Does my helper have a real burning desire to become an artist? He wondered if Urchin was limited by aptitude, limited in his capacity for the many repetitive skills that would go into building craftsmanship. Does he possess a tolerance for error, the patience and dedication necessary for him to blossom from artisan to artist? Does he have the gift of vision necessary for all this, the physical endurance to see his vision realized from the abstract to the concrete? He knew that for some, the endurance necessary to the high altitudes of artistry was lacking and perhaps that would be the trajectory of his student apprentice. *There are hills to climb in this business*—I know because I've trudged my share of them, he thought. Is it fair to ask someone so young to dream of a life in struggle to become an artist? Afri Walker felt Urchin had not pursued this line of thinking, that perhaps he himself should not pursue this avenue with someone so young; but now, in the midst of this new and much welcomed award, this might not be the time to wax philosophical. *There would be time enough for such an exploration. Still, I must ferret out the level of his motivation, must seek to learn the motivation and desire for growth on the part of this one I call Urchin.* The best thing to do is observe— observe how he fastens himself to the task at hand, he thought even as he put the boy down, *fasten him to the task at hand for the time being.*

     For his part, at least in this moment, Urchin had no thought of monetary reward, little understanding of what this would mean in terms of effort and endurance. School had taught him the meaning of assignments, of commitment to learning —at least in the classroom—of modest creativity without controversy, appreciation for a helping guide, and respect for his elders. And his granny had done the best she could with keeping him fed and clothed. He was drawn to the studio because of an adult's willingness to help him earn a few dollars in honest labor. In that way, his apprenticeship—what some at his school called his slavery—had come to him as a benefit. Now, his state of mind was one of mild confusion; this scaffolding, this opportunity to learn at the hand of a Master in the arts of drawing, painting, and perhaps even sculpture was all new to him. When asked the whys and wherefores of his time spent in the studio on Main Street, he fumbled in answering questions about his short-lived engagement. Why you be going down there all the time? You just getting used, slave! You think you be some big time apprentice, but you ain't nuttin' but a slave, ratting out on us, you done left us on the limb mein, you done forgot about your homies! He did in fact feel as though he had abandoned his friends, saw that they felt that they could no longer depend on him as one of them, as one to be protected by them, feared by others who might no longer see him as one of Las Siestas, or at the very least as one courted by the Siestas as a recruit. And some of this was true. He purposely left school quickly taking backstreets downtown, purposely said little about the work he did there and the magic that there transpired, purposely slept in the park sometimes and lied to Granny—I stayed over at LeMarcus' place—and knew that sooner or later the truth would come out. The early weeks of June would be a time of challenge in definition and fortification of purpose in his mind.

Afri put the featherbells in an old vase that had seen duty as a holder of paint brushes; chips of old paint and smells of turpentine decked its personae in the studio. It was effective because it held water. His own apprenticeship had primarily come in reading. Books on John Quincy Adams Ward, Michelangelo, Van Gogh, Rubens, Bearden, and Catlett had been his windows into the past. They along with Leroy Gaskins, an artist friend of his uncle in Washington D.C., served as his inspiration during summer visits. He was essentially self-trained except for that senior year award he'd won which took him to

Italy on a summer stipend. Two months with Florence as his base and travel to Paris and Rome had opened his eyes to the wonders of Europe's artistic past and the possibilities it held for an American future. His training held many holes, but many of his questions in technique could be solved through experimentation, curiosity, endurance, and adaptation; he copied and drew photographs and paintings using both left and right hands with a vengeance. If it can be photographed, it can be drawn and painted, he said to himself. And his work reflected a style that was individual, unique and arresting; his voice had become singular and forceful; in him curiosity and creativity fused. Ahead lay a masterpiece—he felt that in his bones—and his contusions in words and sketches fiddled upon that irksome but menacing little folktale. Those suggestive contusions of work yet to be done heralded a concrete piece which lay in stealth just around the corner. He fish-eyed this ragamuffin of words in this moment:

In this version Curiosity's Idea is on a hunt and runs across a firebird's feather. The Idea's horse warns Idea not to touch it, as bad things will happen. Idea ignores the advice and takes it to bring back to Curiosity so he will be praised and rewarded. When Curiosity is presented with the feather he demands the entire firebird or the death of Idea. Idea weeps back to his horse who instructs him to put corn on the fields in order to capture the firebird. The firebird comes down to eat allowing Idea to capture the bird. When Curiosity is presented with the firebird he demands that Idea fetch the Princess Controversy so that

Curiosity may marry her, otherwise Idea will be killed. Idea goes to the Controversy's lands and drugs her with a wine to bring her back to Curiosity. Curiosity was pleased and rewarded Idea, however when Controversy awoke and realized she was not home she began to weep. If she was to be married she wanted her creative masterpiece, which was (in her mind's eye) under a rock in the middle of the Blue Sea. Once again Idea wept to his horse and fulfilled his duty to Curiosity and brought back the masterpiece. Controversy was stubborn and refused to marry Curiosity even with her masterpiece until Idea was dipped in boiling water. Idea begged to see his horse before he was boiled and the horse put a spell on the Idea to protect him from the water. Idea came out more handsome than anyone had ever seen. Curiosity saw this and jumped in as well but was instead boiled alive. Idea was chosen to be Curiosity and married Controversy and they lived happily.

Based on his Southern roots, Afri knew that many blacks from the Deep South would not respond and would not speak when addressed directly; only when addressed indirectly would an answer be forthcoming. Occasionally, he noticed that trait in his apprentice. He decided on two things; one, to sketch his duties and exercises out on paper and two, he decided to be observe Urchin's caliber of energy—both physical and intellectual—in response to his own. His modest experience in teaching had taught him to observe physical energy and the levels at which it matched his own. Okay Urchin, he said, How do you feel about your apprenticeship? Me? Said Urchin. Yes, said Afri not looking at him directly, You! Well, I like it—I mean, I'm learning stuff—how you draw and check for perspective, how you train your eyes and coordinate your hands, and how you combine certain colors, shade and create shadows. Sometimes, though all my chores get on the way of me practicing and doing my real work, my exercises —you know, like uh, sketching and carving my puppets. But I know that I am not paying for these lessons, and I understand that you have given me an opportunity to learn. Do you feel like you are a slave? said Afri. Well some of my homies tease me about that—say I am a slave to you—but uh, I tell them that I am learning stuff too.

Afri responded slowly saying, You know that area called Fort Pickering, some call it French Fort—you know where I'm talking about? Yeah, said Urchin, I go there sometimes to sit under a tree, a big magnolia tree. Afri said, Yes, I know the one; it's very beautiful. Well there used to be a fort there called Fort Pickering. It was built by black refugees during the Civil War. Those slaves didn't have the chance to think for themselves or even defend themselves before the war; but they sure as hell did a ton of thinking when the war started and they left plantations in droves seeking shelter in the four or five contraband camps around Memphis. Now many of them had no experience in designing books, writing music, or making pieces of sculpture; but they were strong forefathers and we have this opportunity to honor the fighters that went before us—that fought, taught, cooked, sewed, black-smithed, hoed cotton, and worked their tails off to survive. That fort was destroyed after the Civil War. These days, we also have the opportunity to sweat according to our own choices and be rewarded for both our own labor and thought. Since we are beyond both slavery and segregation, we have the responsibility to develop our own models of character and career choices. If you think you want to become an artist or painter or sculptor, I need you to match my energy; can you do that? Yes, I think so, said Urchin thinking, *I don't really know.*

Well I didn't mean to lecture you, but I wanted to chat about that. This commission means a lot of hard work and I do want to be fair; I do want you to help me around the studio this summer. Tell you what, discuss it with your Granny and let me know if I need to talk to her. Let me know too, if your homies bother you—seems to me like they are more of a gang than friends. Yes Master Afri, I said, I will. I've seen those old guys in my neighborhood waiting around big burn-barrels of wood in the wintertime—waiting for this white person or that one to pick them up for yard work and carting stuff around on pickup trucks; don't want no parts of that. I thought I would ask you about talking to Miss Ramona—ask her if she would model for one of my puppets. I figure I would need a photo and maybe she could sit once or twice. That way I could get started on *my* masterpiece. That is a great idea Urchin, said Afri. We'll look into finding a contest, have that piece judged. If you are recognized, that would put you on the road to having a career, a successful career perhaps as an artist. Either way though, you will profit in your work ethic —the pride that you take both in the sweat of your work and the finished product, if you stick with me this summer. I will talk to Ramona about it; try to get a picture for starters. Here, I found this article on John Quincy Adams Ward; he did that sculpture on the wall, The Freedman. His master was Henry Kirke Brown, a sculptor in New York City. Now Ward started out as a paying student with Brown, became his apprentice and then his assistant. He learned his craft—took him seven years, but you can see how Brown's love for the American scene is reflected in his work and the work of Ward. I want this new piece, this piece for the Brinks Gallery, to reflect my appreciation for Ward and a contemporary British sculptor by the name of Damien Hirst.

Thank you Mr. Afri, I noticed your drawings over there; have you chosen a final design for the sculpture, decided which of them is your favorite? Almost Urchin, almost, said Afri. I've been studying the anatomy of birds and reading up on what they call lost wax technique. I used that process in making M3 but I want to alter my tactics, my technique a bit. Like I said, I want to revamp the furnace to keep the bronze hot for a longer period of time. You can take a gander at this information on the technique; you might have some ideas that help me. The sprues and vents were what gave me a fit last time—so really, I am focusing on two things, avian physiology and sprues to vent hot metal. I'm going to sculpt two models in plaster. I thought at first I might do it in wood, but I'm thinking that Plaster of Paris would give us better detail in the feathers. I want you to cross-reference the sprues with me—double up on that because that process has to be done correctly; otherwise, the whole sculpture will really be seen an art class working with plaster of Paris *and man, dust was flying all over the place!* Afri smiled inwardly too; his thoughts ran along the similar but more elaborate lines; *Golly, so we need to get the air-conditioner checked, old Ramona going to be around —with her fine self—springtime is closing out and summertime, when the fish are jumpin', is upon us, and we can dust some magic 'round this place!*

XIII

Those early summer days were ones of luminous sunshine and personal exhilaration for me. Afri had spoken with Ramona and she had agreed to visit the studio at midday for no more than an hour and a half. That way she could address whatever issues broiled at the gallery in the early portion of the day, model and visit with us for a bit, and then resume her post at the gallery to finish up her business day. Many of our discussions and casual talks revolved around mastery, the tireless polishing of an artist's chosen vision, the effort involved in bringing vision to life. Afri said, Ramona tell me why you brought in that mediator to run the meeting of your Board of Directors, don't you usually head those up? Yes Afri I do, but this time Hargrove had discussed the new wing, sabotaged the discussion secretly, planting sensitive questions and hardcore responses with some board members. I needed the group to have a balanced and honest discussion that got fair responses to the whole business of inclusion, of broadening the ethnic diversity of our gallery holdings. Some of our meetings have been disastrous on that issue—almost like a gangland shooting—folks leaving pissed off, despondent, ready to resign at the drop of a hat. We had to have a measured, balanced, unbiased and fruitful discussion. Everybody had to participate and give concrete, written responses to be sure that the entire group was on board with our next moves. *Put that answer in your brain files, compare it with the way Las Siestas operates*; I filed that answer under *save-for-future-reference!*

Here are some sandwiches, ham, tuna, and egg—she said, lugging her laptop and some folders. I'd organized my desk in such a way that she could work there, as I sketched and revised her features on my princess puppet, modeled upon her physique. How do you like this one I'm working on to represent the king? I used some characteristics of Afri's face to make him, only he's much heavier and chunkier than my Master. Aha, she said, I think I recognize Afri in there somewhere—I see penetrating eyes, strong shoulders, muscular forearms; and yes, he is much stockier, fatter than Afri, she said laughing. He's had far too many apple pies to eat! All kings should have apple pies on a regular basis, said Afri, overhearing the comment and adding, Perhaps you should make the king a queen or a cat, then equipoise and gender balance in equal-time would permeate this puppet show. The memory of that comment now sends a slight chill down my spine, as I think of it. It brings an especially frightening episode to mind; one of a pussy cat seen on the way from Riverside Park and more fully exposed the subterranean emotions of Zorro. I suspected him of being the one gang member assigned the task of defining and revealing to the others my summer routine. But yet again, I get ahead in my storytelling and apologize for deviating from a logical path.

The public never sees all the invisibles—the circles, ellipses, tracks of energy, and lines of repetitions it takes to chase mastery, said Afri, Your muscles could ache, rattle, and roll, but they will never know the energy that goes into all that eye to hand syncing, those miscellaneous motions done at varied speeds. Then you have the slicing, chiseling, carving, sketching, polishing, and sanding, not to mention accuracy in dimension, said Afri as Ramona sat posing for me. Yes Afri, but they can see if the final product looks real, or sounds moving or idiotic, said Ramona, Think about that poor princess—in her native land, she was an accomplished seamstress, she had embroidered this dress, now at the bottom of the sea but which started in her mind's eye, as an abstract vision. Or even Ward—let me read you this quote of his words.

> I shall send tomorrow or next day a plaster model of a figure we call the Freedman for want of a better name, but I intend it to express not one set free by any proclamation so much as by his own love of freedom and a conscious power to brake things.

Ramona and Afri both complimented me on the development of the head of the puppet, though it took me several attempts to get the result I was looking for. During periods of frustration, I read and duplicated illustrations on bird anatomy and human anatomy; this included details on the construction of wings, legs, muscles and bones. In fact, I made many sketches of the skeletal structure of birds, gradually adding organs, muscles, skin, and feathers. I did this with both hands and measured my results with micrometers, to test the accuracy of my manipulations. My, my Urchin, said Ramona as she leafed through my pencil sketches and traces, you're getting better all the time Urchin, Your Master best watch out, lest you better him! She'd brought dust masks for us that day and occasionally she would wear jeans and help me sweep and mange studio debris. Afri had put an advertisement in the Commercial Flyer to get word of my quills about town. The sale of those quills will boost your income Urchin—you have a good idea there and it should benefit you handsomely. Ramona took some quills to the gift shop at the gallery; I was quite pleased with the prices they fetched and occasionally she would bring me notes of encouragement written with those quills; her words gave me sparkles of joy that glow to this very day!

    It would be untruthful to say that I had not been overtaken by a maddening crush on her; her poise and beauty, her patient demeanor, and her sensitive manner of conversing with both of us, though I did notice her eyes follow Afri as he shifted gears in sculpting, polishing, and chiseling the vision he had for his masterwork of the Firebird. Afri became stronger as he worked, both in spirit and physically. Even the furnace workers commented that he seemed infused with a religious fervor, inspired by all that negative space only seen by him. I see what you are after in the revealing of layers in your sculpture, Ramona would say, or, The arcing wing looks as if it, like—might leave the rest of the plaster piece fastened, blocked where it stands! Try as I might, I had a difficult time in the manufacture of energy matching the fury in which he worked. Perhaps fury is not the exact word, since his was a disciplined fury—at times slow and industrious and at others, closely akin to that of molten lava, hot and fiery! To this day, I have no idea of how my address was found, but in the second or third week of summer I received the following note, penned by the hand of Hargrove the critic, which I hid from my Master but which caused me both pride and grief.

Dear Monsieur Urchin:

    I am a great admirer of your feather quills used for writing. Just yesterday one of your quills came to my attention through a friend. Also mentioned was your apprenticeship with artist and sculptor Afri Walker. I have a great curiosity to learn more of your craftsmanship and as you see am in ownership of one of your writing instruments. I look forward to discussing with you the details of this business venture and take this opportunity to request a few moments of your time, to interview you with regard to the details of this enterprise. Additionally, I should like to purchase several more of these well crafted tools. Please feel free to contact me at 901-704-9796.

    Very cordially,

    Wesley Hargrove

Needless to say, I hid this missive from my Master and showed it to no one. The memory of my Master's joy in peppering the review given by this critic of his MemNoire was fresh in my memory and my joy in receiving these words of praise and interest stood in direct opposition to his anger and disgust. I am loathe to admit that my bamboo gun remained at rest in my pocket. The grief comes in recognizing that this note caused a subtle shift in attitude, caused me surreptitious egotism, caused me to subtlety resent infractions on my time and focus, caused me to falsely elevate myself in esteem and sense my apprenticeship false. When asked by my Master, Well Urchin, what do you think of this Firebird? I coyly responded, Well Mr. Afri, do you not think that the wings should be balanced—to give it a more classical look. If Fergus were here, he might prefer that sketch where you have the Firebird perched above the earth with a flag or featherbells in its beak—almost as if the whole were a musical note. If the truth be told, I waxed a bit annoyed with all that rotating axis, stark asymmetry, peeling of muscle, detailed organ and bone structure. My own poor results representing a rotating axis in my puppets prevented the most elementary thoughts of rendering muscle, bone, or organs in my puppets. Much to my chagrin, I blurted, I wish I could come up with some of the concepts you manage to concoct. Were I Ms. Ramona, I should think that some featherbells would dangle from its beak! I think he was mildly confused by that remark; he rarely asked for my comments on his progress for a few days.

In the meantime, I made a picture-walk, a storyboard, and a cartoon of the firebird folktale; they formed simple representations of the tale and were simple enough for my friends to read and understand, even Bay Brother. In reality, I think I was beginning to miss my friends, the carefree manner in which they caroused the Memphis streets, their gangsta jargon, and the ease with which they teased one another. Imagine my surprise when Afri asked, Do you miss your friends Urchin? Miss hanging out and blowin' navy beans at passing trains? You don't seem to talk about them much. What about your grades—did you pass to the twelfth grade? I don't remember much about how I answered that question, but I do remember what happened to the cat.

From time to time, I had the feeling that I was being followed on my way to the Main Street studio. Of course I took precautions that would disguise my route, often circling the block on occasion and doubling back in seemingly stupid ways. I had devised a scheme that—in the event I did come across a member of Las Siestas—I would show the story board of my puppet show to whomever I met, so as to explain my absences from neighborhood alliances and affirm my new engagement. For sure, I did not want to meet Zorro; I was afraid he would catch me in a lie, figure out some crazy ambush, and configure some bizarre reprisal. If I did meet someone from the gang, I hoped that it would be Bay Brother as he was the most lovable of the group. It would be fairly easy to chat with him and give him some jumbled description of what I was up to, describe it to him in really confusing ways, that my life had changed—that I had changed—and that being a gang member was now the most distant association I could possibly think of. Events with other folk rarely come about as we imagine them; in my case this was true beyond doubt's wildest affectations. As fate would have it, LeMarcus was the one I first encountered after imagining all this.

Where you been lil' bro—we thought you had just upped and died? Me—no, been around, I said. Around *where* Urchin—heard that is what they call you now, Urchin right? said LeMarcus. I said, Hey, brother LeMarcus, I gets called a bunch of thangs—homie mostly, just like y'all always used to do, but my boss likes Urchin, so that be another one of them. LeMarcus smiled, Urchin it is then, Urchin. Anyway —*Urchin*—we been stopping by your granny's crib lookin' for you, checking streets north and south...seeing if anybody done seen you, scouring here and there, and all of a sudden, here you be! Somebody said you had a new job, so we kinda gave up—not all the way, just kinda. Man, it's *so* good to see you and looking prosperous too, even with all this summer heat jackin up the place. Yeah, thought you had dissolved! Well we found each other and that's a good thing, I said tapping my pocket for my cartoon crutch. Look, we gon' check out Riverside Park later tonight, see if we can catch up on some old times, smoke a blunt, light up some rats, kick it you understand. Couple of the other guys got jobs too, so its been hard to get everybody together, get the boys on the same page, make sure that we keep up with one another. Just as I was about to break out my crutch, my story-board, Zorro walked up.

Well I'll be, said Zorro. Was this was a planned interception or happenstance? I thought. I left the storyboard in my pocket, said, Zo baby, whassup blood, and scanned LeMarcus, Yeah, that sounds good, sounds real dope Zo. LeMarcus—I'll bring that stuff I borrowed from you tonight. Okay—Gotta help my granny around the house a bit, you know, grass cuttin' and shit. Been outa pocket for a minute! I shot a chin-nod to Zorro. How you be bro? Solid man, s'all good, said Zorro. I could feel LeMarcus givin' me the twice-over, checking out my reactions and sweat-levels real close; scanning for beeps in my tension meter. Heard you had a new gig, said Zorro, stepping in real close; joy rolled through his face like a sleigh at Xmas time; he used invasion-of-personal-space as his fear thermometer. Why you stepping so close to him, Zorro—he gots to have air just like everybody else, said LeMarcus. Zorro stepped back, his hands out wide and open, feigning as if encroachment was miles from his mind. Oh—I forgot—you be his guardian angel or somethin'. LeMarcus what time? I said, dousing the souring interaction, I want to be sure I get everything done Granny needs. Look for us round about seven, LeMarcus said. If I don' show, Bay Brother will. Oh by the way, said Zorro, his voice in silky mode, Saw you comin' from up there on the hill, the same way you walk to your Grans' house. Left something—a gift—up there for your eyes, seeing as how you *abandoned* us lately...forgot to check on your homies. We be left high and dry *mein*.

The hill was more like a slope, but I said, Okay, and stepped away softly so as to hear any moves behind me. At the end of the slope, I turned the corner to Granny's; the pussy cat there still kicked and jiggled, climbing with both feet, lurching for air, its neck secured by rope, the rope lynched to a tree. In the distance, *Zorro yelled, That's what happens to rats, muther...ker! Seven,* said LeMarcus, holding up seven fingers, Don't forget your beer money! Bring your gas can, yelled Zorro.

Granny sat in her rocker when I arrived at the house; she used her walking stick to make the rocker rock and the place smelled close and of her fragrance. Boy lil' bit of everybody's been here lookin' fur you, she spoke sideways because of the tobacco; I gits tired trying to figure jus' wha you is doing, where you be or anything else 'bout you. Your moma asked to raise you up right—asked me to *faithfully attend,* her head bobbing on those last two words. I nodded, went to my room, changed shirts, returned and said, I love you Granny. Then I cranked the lawn mover, cut the grass, front and back so as to use all the gas, and washed out the can for later. Granny could still kick after the first stroke; after the second, she couldn't do much.

Hey Bay Brother, I said when the knock came on the door, You talk with Zorro and LeMarcus? Uh-huh, said Bay Brother. Those fools told me you were comin' along, told me you were anxious to hang out—thought you had a new job? I do but I haven't seen y'all for a good while, I said. I'm ready for a little fun; looky here...wanted to show you a story-board, a picture walk through a puppet show I'm putting together. No shit, you making a puppet show? said Bay Brother, I loves them puppet shows...seen 'em on TV, saw one at school too. His eyes bugged, You gettin' better wid your drawings. He whispered, Don't forget your beer money, so Granny wouldn't hear him. I said, Solid homes, I been practicing like crazy —both hands too, just like on the court. Bay Brother was pretty good at basketball, but his dribbling was like his reading—sub par. The only one among us who had access to a car was LeMarcus; we headed to his house and I carried the can. Zorro and Parrot were already there, along with two new guys I didn't know.

LeMarcus' dad walked us out to the beat up Buick and said, You boys be careful drivin' 'round town. Been a bunch of hooligans shootin' up Poplar Plaza and creatin' mayhem on weekends. I hear 'bout any crap and LeMarcus loses drivin' privileges. Like I said, his dad was a big, muscular guy, so we all said Yessir! in unison. Nobody said much as we started and a weird tension ruled. Once, while we started jaw-jackin' driving down to Tom Lee Park, LeMarcus had back-handed Zorro for hollerin' about his driving—Pow!—before Zorro even saw the fist comin'. That back-hand managed to keep Zorro's mouth shut for a good, long time. Now, as we headed to Riverside, our discussions went from silence to raggedy to feisty. When we were a block away, I said, I got gasoline and beer money. LeMarcus said, The cops will be watchin' wid all these brothers in the car, we best break up once we get to the park entrance. We be free, we can drive wherever the hell we want! said a dufus-lookin' dude, his hat pulled down over his eyes. Not a great idea, said Bay Brother. I agree, said Zorro, breaking his silence; he leaned forward saying, Once we buy the beer, we put everything in the trunk. All of us get out and walk through the park to the landing area. LeMarcus can meet us there and then we start the party...what you think LeMarcus? That'll work, said LeMarcus, that'll work! I kept my mouth shut while we headed down to MLK Park, taking South Parkway past Kansas, four of us in the backseat.

    We stopped at a MAPCO station to fill up my portable gas can; Zorro copped the beer. A huge, black and shiny Hummer H3 swung in right behind us. I guess my nerves were a bit jangled, 'cause the thump and boom of the bass and wheeze of the windows made me jump. A faint breeze of marijuana floated from its windows and long-legged Martians slid from its doors. Rap music by Smutt Merchant oozed from one half-opened door as I pumped gas; not one speck of dust clung to the gleam of its black exterior. I paid my bill and hopped in; Zorro did his thing and closed the trunk. Man, I could take a picture off the reflections on dat Hummer—Jeez! All eyes were riveted to the Hummer. We rode close enough to walk to MLK Park and everybody got out to walk except LeMarcus. LeMarcus said, See y'all inside, and we ambled down the road to the old Riverside Park entrance. Bay Brother said, Y'all got ya bamboo—Ow! Before he could finish, Zorro had tagged him real good with pellets from his blow gun. Sorry sucker, told you you ain't in charge, you ain't never gon' be in charge stupid mufuc—r! Just shut your mouth and walk, goddammit—ain't nobody got time fur—Wham! The brogan had flown by me like a jet-stream and caught Zorro in the crack of his butt. I'd noticed that the sound of our feet made arrhythmical sounds, not the sounds of old, which struck the pavement in unisons, sounds which felt like the unity of a team. Hey guys c'mon—we sposed ta be having fun, and everyone rushed to restrain Bay Brother from putting something real serious on Zorro. Zorro brushed off his pants saying, That one will cost you bro, cost you.

XIV

The sun was setting on Ole Man River when we reached Riverside Park, now called MLK. LeMarcus pulled his dad's '89 Buick into a parking spot and we double checked the gas can, putting it inside a big green garbage bag and then a plastic freezer box. Kids played and giggled in the play area as we walked and waved to onlooking hand-holders, beer drinkers and landscape lovers; sunsets, late May and June do that to people, make them puppets to the magic of that blazing, fiery sun closing out the day. *Puppets on a string,* I mused, thinking of my puppets alone in the studio. LeMarcus signaled the direction, Zorro led the way once he had spotted a remote fifty-five gallon open barrel, nestled behind a stand of huge oak trees majestic in their tower over debris washed up on the shoreline. Man, said one of the twins, silent riders whose hats had finally risen up enough to show surly faces. You could die up in here and never be found. N-n-n-never be found, said Parrot coming to life, And don' think that s-s-sh-shit ain't happened! Never be found, he whispered. Zorro went over to the open barrel, studied it for a minute and then came over to me. Urchin my brother, fetch that gasoline can out of the freezer box and let me hold it for a minute or two. Okay, give me a minute, I said.

LeMarcus busied himself with drawing a single line of coat hanger wire across the top of the can and rigging it so that it stretched across the top as if it were BB King's banjo Lucille—minus the other strings. Out in the deep part of the Mississippi, you could see a huge barge pushed upstream by a tugboat. Man, I thought they would be glad to see you, said Bay Brother, and Zorro act like he madder than shit, LeMarcus come and go like he on his period. I said, Not to worry Bay. That anger comes from a real deep place that only they know about; Zorro been angry and f—edup all his life like that; LeMarcus, well something must be going down at the house. Bay Brother took the beer back to the anointed spot, I carried the gas can. I noticed that Zorro took several long yellow things out of his pocket, pasted them with peanut butter, and stuffed the concoction into a red Texsun grapefruit can; the wire ran through the can and he angled a foot wide wooden ramp up against the barrel. Oh man, we gon' have some real fun tonight, 'specially when the darkness comes down, Zorro said. The other two dudes sat on the slope of the river's edge, drawing on joints they had already rolled and Bay Brother busied himself rolling marijuana into a blunt. Homes, Clint—everytime I roll one of these I gits it all screwed up; guess my fingers are jus' way too big. Big fingers are a good thing big brother; folk know beforehand that you pack a whallop. Bay Brother hadn't called me Clint in years. Your boy there knows it and be wondering what it feels like to get knocked into the next century, I said. He laughed.

    I moseyed over to where Zorro was, put the gas can on the ground, looked out at the setting sun for a bit, stepped to Zorro, and said, You act like you want a piece of me Zorro; if that's the case then this is the time. I kept my hands in my pockets and stood just out of his reach, in case he had a knife. I had something in my pockets that was a little heavier than a knife, but had no trigger. I had brought it along just in case I needed to fake it. LeMarcus looked at us from just beyond earshot, wondering what we were talking about, a wide smirk riding longways across his face. *From over here, looks like y'all bout to get it on my brothers. I know we be jacking and talkin' shit, but it ain't 'sposed to get that serious like y'all be lookin'; that ain't bout what Las Siestas be about.* When I stop to think about it now, the words used in the hood amounted to repeats and between lines, words said where the meaning happened in the intonation, not in dictionary definitions or gray vocabularies. *Truth on a slide-rule has colors too!* Where did that come from? I wondered. Was it because black jargon had been stolen and gentrified? Deep down, I understood the energy and reality of encrypted intonations. Old-timers said cool *used* to mean to *not show* emotion, now it meant *okay*; *weird*.

Bay Brother cracked open two beers, tossed a closed one to LeMarcus and the same to Zorro, handed an open one to me and kept the other. The two quiet guys came down and pulled up beside LeMarcus. Nobody asked questions, since to ask questions was to get in a body's business: *inappropriate.* To not ask question was to dis another: *why you be disrespecting me, bro?* Either way, you were in for an ass-kicking, which was the whole point. To show you where you reside in the hierarchy; to give you what you didn't ask for whenever you do or don't ask for it! That was the rule of the hood, that was the rule of the gang. *Did that happen in Ramona's Board of Directors? I thought theirs was the cultured society. But then the papers say that Republicans be dissing the President. What the fuck kind of civilized culture is that?* Zorro shocked me from my day-mare, saying A toast to la Siesta—one for all, and the group chorused, and all for one! I was reading about your new boss in the papers Urchin, reading 'bout ch'all and shit. *There it is again, the double pump, double-pump back*, I said, alright, alright! *I thought to ask is that double pump meant to take up space, convince me that you are serious, show me that you can read, lure me by your forthrightness...just why are you saying the same words twice*—Lil' brother, I said, I was lucky enough to get a gig, real lucky to meet a guy that is training —, helping me to work on some skills, become an apprentice! Is that a problem?

I didn't know what the relationship, the real relationship of these two no-names to Zorro, but now for some reason, intuition told me they were related to him, short physiques, stubby noses, ratlike eyes—but their manner was different—almost inverts of his manner, repressed where he was bold and authoritative, like a king barking orders. *Where an archer would weep and beg, the king orders fetching, capture, and hauling. But do you want to be a king? he asked himself.* LeMarcus held out his arm to extinguish their movement; not only did I see that, but

Bay Brother flinched since he did also. Just then the sun seemed to stand on its last embers. Everybody all tense and shit—was this all about—is somebody jealous? said Bay Brother. *Exactly, I thought.* No problem, said Zorro, Hell no, ain't no problem even in it, sure as hell ain't got shit to do wid jealousy, I mean after all he ain't no bitch—is he? Bay Brother held out his arm to hold me back and handed me a blunt: I lit it, took a few cool puffs, inhaled very deeply, took a swig of my beer, looked off into the last peeps of sunset and said, F—k you Zorro!

Tell you what, said Zorro, I think we do have a problem, since you be dissing on me—Did you say dissing or pissing? Said Bay Brother. Again, I wondered if Ramona's meetings were anything like this; *damn! Ain't nobody talking to you! Reddish embers from all the joints and blunts fired up at that point twittering like little fireflies in the darkness.* Anyway, like I was sayin' I propose that we mount a shooting contest with bamboo guns to start, and he rose, to pour gasoline into the open barrel trash can, and took out his bamboo gun, to see who can hit that can on top of that open barrel, hit that burn barrel over yonder. Just a 'lil contest to see who be the better shooter. The navy beans be right here and the bamboo gun pledge means everybody got their guns in their pockets. Bay Brother took a deep breath saying, You got your gun? Always, I said, adding, Do I need the real thing? You nuts? he said adding, I brought my slingshot, just in case. Bamboo blow guns appeared all around. Now, just to make the ante a little more interesting, lets just wait a minute or two for the rats to come up for that cheese I put inside the horizontal can; you knock 'em off into the barrel and we got ourselves a righteous lil party! And we'll light those mouf—rs right up! And sure enough, right while we sat there, drinking beer and smoking joints, rats the size of kitty cats started sneaking up the ramp Zorro put on the side of the burn barrel, trying to tackle the cheese and peanut butter. *A trap!*

Well navy beans started whizzing through the air like arrows in a Robin Hood movie, with folks taking deeper and deeper breaths to get more speed. Those rats would turn, look, scamper down the ramp, and then start up again. Y'all twins better start shootin' better, y'all shoot like a bunch of sissies, yelled Zorro. That was another indication for me that he'd brought his mini-posse with him; Bay caught it too and looked at me with a broad grin. So far, not a one had fallen in the burn barrel, that was until Bay Brother brought out his sling shot, right away one fell in with a *thonk*, and then another. One of the twins blew his cover, and cranked a BB pistol; he got one more to fall in and then a coupla more. Zorro ran over and lit the can with a match. Amid the din of rats trying to leapfrog outta there, a huge plume of smoke and fire rocketed from that can, lighting up the immediate shoreline like the Fourth of July. One rat made it out, hauled ass down into the river and took flight like it was a firebird come to life, its coat and full anatomy ablaze with hellish fury. In the distance, a single then multiple sirens could be heard screeching over the low hum of passing traffic. Zorro ran to get rope from the car, threw the rope over a tree and balanced himself in an awkward attempt to lasso one of the rats; excited as he ran back, he stumbled up against the gas can, kicked it over and loosed a stream of leftover gas down towards the burn barrel. Another plume of gas rose, roared, and flared: the plume reared like a red seahorse rocketing from his foot. LeMarcus covered his face from the heat, Bay Brother gasped, the twins gaped and Parrot squawked, Roll over, man, r-r-rrroll the fuck over! Bay heard the sirens, turned to me and said, Ain't never learned to follow orders, always giving 'em! We need to bounce! I knew how to get to the golf course, but not in the dark. We split at full speed, right after LeMarcus ran for the car. The twins threw beer and mud on Zorro's foot and pants, yelling Roll over man, roll over! I heard the roar, then spotted the flash of blue lights of sirens hauling ass in our direction and yelled to Bay Brother, Bay, Bay—we need to bounce man, get the hell outta here!

Help, help, screamed Zorro, Parrot screamed, Roll over fool, roll—! That way, I said to Bay Brother, through those bushes. We ran, hauled ass all the way to French Fort, chugging and puffing, laboring like mad locomotives; by the time we reached pavement, it felt like our shoe bottoms were on fire, not to mention being totally out of breath. Walk for a minute, panted Bay. Yeah, I said. We walked for a block, then broke into a trot, heading for the Old Marine Hospital up by the Cherokee Mounds; then we lay down flat in the park, behind the mounds. Better split up Urchin, said Bay Brother, damn I'm tired. Yeah, I said, figuring that the police cars screaming in back of us were cruising the area to find anything looking like it had been down in the park. He left heading east while I waited, and circled back around the motels to that old magnolia that I loved.

I wondered if Zorro had realized that he was king-like, ordering folk, insisting on being slave master, refusing mediation, refusing peace-pipe equity, a blackened imitation of oft found Caucasian ego and hubris; always right, always white, always on the gossip, research end, but rarely in action on behalf of those around him. Granny would often mention say, there goes some Tuskegee taffy, in reference to some new plot, designed to ingratiate her behavior she styled trickish; her most treasured volume was an old dusty book around the house which chronicled the Tuskegee experiment. That book looked as if it had been read a thousand times; white folk always *studying* the Negro, but when it comes to education and economics—the things that would truly help him to *compete*—their actions speak way louder than their words. John Brown would turn over in his grave, she said. Perhaps where black folk are now, I mused, like the archer in the folktale, had to be creative to survive death, and when the slave master has to compete, to jump in the boiling water, he and his progeny die. All because the king tried to compete with creativity; and the critic, old Hargrove, wants to *harvest* that creativity. Ramona acts as if, thinks as if, cultural institutions have failed black folk, I surmised. Then my thoughts turned to Bay Brother and LeMarcus, wondering if they made it home, wondering how bad Zorro was burned, wondering about those twins and their quiet seething, wondering where Parrot ended up! Then I rolled over under that old magnolia tree and fell asleep dreaming of giant red seahorses galloping across the Mississippi.

XV

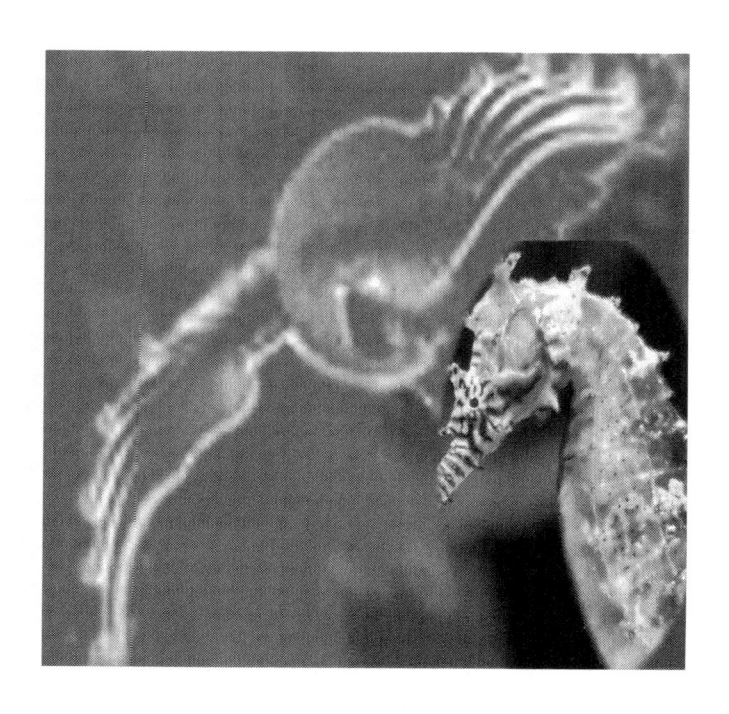

A phantom! I reached up to touch it, an oversized red-rich seahorse floating suspended over the Mississippi River, right at the Memphis bluffs. Behind the specter stood bituminous clouds, scattering from blasts of lightning in the strobed, streaked sky. Thunder barked in lunges, bellowing down the valley between bridges, shattering the peace and patter of gentle rain. The phantom seahorse, a gelatinous string-free puppet, floated like a hummingbird. Beacons of light beamed from its scalloped, diamond-shaped eyes as they scanned the bluffs and bridges of the Memphis skyline. Occasionally, the thing would spin its lustrous, scaled anatomy revealing interiors akin to stained-glass windows. Its skin, at once translucent and transparent, ingested shards of lightning, spinning them forth as webs of ruby light dusted upon maroon waters. No fortuitous boom unhinged the Seahorse's pose. Gamboled by deafening thunder-shocks, its internal gyroscope gently recaptured poise. Airborne, the phantom moved in exact opposition to my instincts, its back arched stiff in perpetual prance. *I heard but could not taste, tasted but could not smell, smelled but could not see, saw but could not touch, felt but could not move.* My mouth emitted soundless screams, blew breaths without velocity, compelled my body with naught for a response.

Below, in the flatlands of parks and bluffs, rats clad in blue and gray skirmished and scrimmaged, scouring for military advantage. The seahorse bobbled in mid-wind, yet hardy in its foreign habitat. Wagons and cavalry wheeled in columns and ranks, colliding in nuggets of guerrilla warfare seeking the destruction of one another, screaming orders, firing sparkles of grape and Minnie-balls in fierce attempts to dislodge nests and spidery webs of resistance. The phantom shifts position, its rubicund anatomy pulsing in flushes of fuchsia, crimson, and puce. I reached again to touch the hovering giant, investigate its skin, interrogate its presence, annoyed by its mute witness to the fury of warring rats in mad scatter of mutual annihilation. *Does wind arrest my movement?* Now armies of rats in white burn crosses, lynch black rats in leers and rituals of sacrifice and demonic festival. *I heard but could not taste, tasted but could not smell, smelled but could not see, saw but could not touch, felt but could not move.* Swirls of dust curled in fierce funnels gouging craters, rogue avenues, and planting slivers of splintered tree limbs in the bluffs. Veins of varicose flashes ignited by Igor's Infernal Dance screamed like arrowheads in flurries of primal screams.

Thunderous booms shook my feet; I groped air for balance as tremors uprooted my toes. Crimson showers morphed to white, gold, and mint flashing cloves of warriors and guerrillas mounted on the wind. Bleached skeletons marched beyond fractured bluffs bearing briefcases. I found no channel to motion, no avenue to personal focus that caused any part of my own anatomy to action; this apparition held me transfixed in an arrested box of witness. Peculiar in their mid-southern geography, tornadoes skipped around the bluffs of Memphis, sidelined, rolled-up at their flanks by prevailing north winds accelerated by the valley, the bluffs, the wide expanse of water at Delta's doorway.

Serenity infected this calm talisman! This horse of the sea blazed colorful in flagrant combinations of greens, reds, golds, and purples, displayed a belly of glass tattooed in sparkling rainbows, its luminous skin festooned in an array of prisms. The greens used reds for flowers, the reds spoke green to grow in showers, as rainbows barnacled to beacons, leaped and danced like trout, sparkling across the bluffs. Skeletons in the flats below unchained their strings and bent their willful backs in heft and heave of feathers and quills; nevermore as string puppets. What do you there with that feather? Dis here be my quill! Celebrate the elemental, consecrate a renaissance, bring to flower this tapestry anew! They flailed and quaked, passing off commentary as communication. The crimson seahorse perched itself further upstream. In response, a blazing rainbow bursts from the saxophone bell standing at the Cannon Center.

A bold incongruity unfolded in the periphery of light. Prints of hooves and feet, left in the cinders and sod on the muddy bluffs, spoke to new covenants made to spur open the doors of cultural institutions, to embrace a unity of humanity beneath the skin.

Skeletons knelt and danced in rituals designed to revoke hierarchies of souls, royalty of birth, ignite tolerance of color, embrace unity of organ and bone. Charmed and minus goose-steps, the trail encircled campfires constructed in clearings loosely made of leaves and twigs. Once again, I exerted my will to seize this crimson talisman, this phantasm far removed from coral waters. My eyes could see but touch and voice were yet tethered far beyond my will. My mouth made no sound, my fingers touched no thing. Skeletons preached at campfires in the valley of the bluffs, vaguely reminiscent of fireflies aglow in fiefdoms forged in yonder Middle Ages. The voices spoke ruefully of Rule by Gold and harped on a Golden Rule. Actions spoke otherwise.

Even as instinct compelled my focus to research, my soul stood magnetized to earth unable to seek out movement; *I heard but could not taste, tasted but could not smell, smelled but could not see, saw but could not touch, felt but could not move.* Lightning reached me far before thunder sounded. Periodically, in times of great peril, the boom and flash would force a huddle of community, but Old Man Culture—one of separation, anxiety, pessimism—waxed static, while dynamic younger feet proclaimed poetic riffs in eloquence profane! Institutions proud and static stood in humble reverence, dominated from the West by ethos borne of finance, shocked by values foreign to its halls. Once hallowed walkways of theology, education, music, dance, and librarian-ship remained ensconced in consonance, faithful to powers of singularity, to theory long abolished by great tests. A dearth of leadership left skeletons adrift. The colors separated leaving voids of imagination within institutions wedded to what *was*; static. Exhausted, I looked at the prevailing winds, I cast a soundless scream. My faithful magnolia stood over me, its limbs shaking and trembling in rain become heavy; something shocked me awake.

Rain had soaked me thoroughly, especially my back. I'd slept face down, my stomach and ribs carried the slatted architecture of the bench; I walked like a mobile music staff, embossed with the notes I'd seen on Fergus' Firebird scores. One or two of those CDs Fergus had left at the studio would have helped me keep my pace, especially Stravinsky's last movement; Berlin had played that the fastest. I had chosen different recordings for each movement, and preferred Philly for the middle, New York for the opening, and Szell's Cleveland for the last. A cold drizzle kept me in an up-tempo walk; every so often I studied the events of the night, the plume of orange smoke, the lynched rats, the special knots tied by Zorro, the academic anger for all things academic that roiled just below the surface in both LeMarcus and Zorro. From time to time, given the perspectives of his dad, I wondered if LeMarcus would end up a Jihadist, his anger, in frequent simmer became explosive in mixed-race situations. I knew in my heart that most urban environments in the 'hood were breeding grounds for Jihadist and would-be terrorists; of course the biggest issue was reading and of course local colleges and universities had no ladder down, no reading improvement presence in the 'hood, either face-to-face or on the Internet. I marveled at their thorough commitment to minimize support for public education. *Did LeMarcus get his car out of the park before the curfew?* The thought nibbled at me as I broke into a trot. The trot did not last long as my legs were wet and sore. The weirdness of my dream teased me as I pressed and flushed my pants against my thighs, freeing them of copious amounts of water. Be great to get to Granny's; she'll be asleep by now and as the thought buoyed my feelings, I noticed that the lights in my neighborhood and on my street were out; the 'hood itself was black as tar and quiet.

    I kept my eyes peeled for angered Siestas and found myself surprised when the outside door opened at my slightest touch. I called for Granny and received no answer. Granny, Granny! I said. Nothing! I went to the kitchen, fumbled for a candle and put the candle on the table. I found a tea towel, dried my hands, and lit a match. The flame sputtered and quivered as I leaned towards the candle and quivered yet again as it brought the candle to life. Candlelight grew to the kitchen's far corner, landing on Granny's favorite rocker. At first I thought Granny was merely asleep; *but she would have locked the door!* My heart raced a little faster now as I whispered Granny, Granny, for a good long time. I shook her and put my cheek to her face; her face was really cold to my touch. I shivered while kneeling to kiss Granny still whispering her name. If death was dark and cold, death had conquered Granny. My own pulse quickened; I became overtaken with strangeness. Granny was dead! The chorus of my dream echoed in me; *I heard but could not taste, tasted but could not smell, smelled but could not see, saw but could not touch, felt but could not move.* Oh my, I thought, Jeez. Granny, Granny!! Except for my cries, the place reposed in silence. I sat in the corner next to Granny's rocker; in this moment I felt truly alone.

     It was a week before I resumed my position at Afri's studio. The sounds of the Firebird Suite reverberated as I entered the studio, bonging old M3. Sorry for your loss, said Afri giving me the once over, Heard you lost your Grandma—read it in the paper—somebody left a program on the door. I had mixed reaction to that revelation, but figured that Bay Brother had left it. Thank you master, I said, examining my puppets and assessing the depth of dust that had collected in my absence. Trills and arpeggiated leaps in the woodwinds and strings punctuated my gaze as I scanned the place; I'd seen these color combinations in my dream. I felt at home, happy to be around the smells and sights of the place, uplifted by the products of my imagination. On auto pilot, I fisted my favorite broom and grabbed a shovel, hefted a wastebasket to and fro to capture debris. The music followed a visually oriented construction of the tale designed for ballet. After minimal cleaning, I gave my attention to my puppets, sanding, carving, and sketching new and enhanced details. Afri came over and put his hand on my shoulder; Urchin, we all have things that happen in life, things that we don't always understand, he said.

Nothing I can say will take the pain away, but you can heal yourself through the magic of your effort; if you match my perspiration with your own, you'll be just fine. A movie of the apprentice about to be dipped in boiling water ran in the back of my mind. And one more thing, he said, I found some maps of bird anatomy that might interest you—somewhere down the line you'll have to get down to business on the bird and away from that beautiful representation of Ramona! Fergus stopped by and left this horse hair for your inspection; he's gonna bring the trio by at some point so you can hear his arrangement, see the violin up close and personal, he added.

      Inwardly I smiled at that; Fergus had complimented both my puppets and quills during his last visit saying, Lil' brother, you're gaining ground on your *big* brother, spurring him on and do...with him chasing John Ward and you stalking our Maestro! My master had tried his hand at casting before. M3 was the result and though flawed, it stood as a testament to the faces it bore and to Afri's commitment to grow as an artist. The final product had taken multiple attempts accomplished through fierce tenacity. Afri walked over to the photo of John Quincy Ward's Freedman, lifting dust from its face with a soft cotton cloth. This time the BONG of M3 startled us both—Hi y'all, Urchin—here take these! As Ramona spoke, she handed me two bouquets of live featherbells, Here—it's so goooood to see you! I heard about your Granny and am so sorry that happened. I have one set of featherbells for you and one for Afri. Here's a hot mocha, one for Afri, you too; and I've got some good news! Before I knew it, a tall vase was in my hands and Ramona had placed a warm kiss on my forehead. Hi Ramona, I said, Good to see you too. I waited to see if she would take a seat in her pose position. Urchin, I can't stay today, we got all kinds of crazy meetings, but I promise to get back on track! She went over to Afri, whispered something in his ear and said, Come over Urchin, I have a letter for Afri and want to share it with you both. Out of her shoulder bag, she pulled out a letter-sized envelop and started reading from parchment contained therein. Blah, blah...hmm...blah...she said, skipping over the printed formal introduction. It is with great pleasure that we award the Director's Choice Award of twenty-five thousand dollars to Afri Walker for a sculpture yet to be named. Afri leapt into the air sparring belatedly with dust. I stepped behind Ramona to read the letter for myself thinking, *the princess fetched her embroidered dress mounted on a Seahorse*; fetched became a word that gained new color for me, one that suggested the chase and seizure of effort through perspiration. When Ramona left, I stood in the doorway, looked across the street, and spotted the graffiti I'd drawn some time ago; instead of the king's crown I had drawn, the blistered crown had become a turban as white as a tuft of cotton.

XVI

A series of nagging aches and neck pains pestered Afri as he chiseled and sculpted the wings of the firebird; he had studied and copied parts of avian anatomy, drafted several one-dimensional composites, afterwards sketching an array of multi-dimensional postures before tackling an initial plaster model. The second model of clay came as an echo to the first. As a courtesy to Ramona, he had shared a bevy of sketches and concepts of posture; they had agreed on two sketches and he'd started work on the models. Occasionally, as a spasm or twitch developed in muscles of his shoulders, back, or arms, he would stop and rest, drinking water or tea. *Man, these feathers just don't look right, they measure correctly, but don't reflect light vividly enough to capture a sense of movement. I need spin in the axis that looks natural, reflects movement, but is open enough on one side to yield a transparent inside to the muscle, sinew, organs, and bones of the skeleton,* he thought. To a witness of his preparation, the recapture of the bird's eyes on paper would have seemed redundant, mechanical, perhaps even boring. Lines, circles, ellipses, were repeated in unending volumes for accuracy and eventual measurement. The exercises would be executed by his own muscles, reflected in them while he extended his legs to chisel, flexed his hands to polish, fisted his fingers and arms to sculpt or flexed palms while investigating the texture of wings with eyes closed. *This wing up and arched– maybe show the keel as bone, fleshy on the other side.* Models peppered the walls of the studio, sketched by his own hand and served as points of refraction, as artificial mirrors reminding him of his concept. Only one real mirror now existed. Later he might remove the sketches and replace each one with real mirrors to help him capture the sketches in multiple dimensions.

    The sculpture of Damien Hirst had fascinated him for the longest; now he wanted to bring an element of that attitude, of an x-ray attitude, to this current project. The spectacular movement of birds of prey in motion, yet still enough to present the opportunity to study its innards—the keel, pectoralis, triceps, and forearms he hoped to show, especially the rope-and-pulley system of the wings. For a second he reflected on his work of the past week, the voluminous sketching, the building of bird limbs in clay and plaster, for he was unsure of the mediums and desired to know which would respond effectively to his conception. His arms and his upper torso were covered with dust, as was his hair. *I should have done this kind of experimentation much earlier—much, much earlier—my sense of how this can be realized evaporates when I give it too much thought.* And he sculpted and chiseled far into the night, nonstop—*catch the vision while it's hot!* His impassioned efforts brought forth two realizations, two concrete visions, equally telling in their capture of the folktale and informing him of the chase on which the firebird was about to embark—*a chase of mastery, yes...a chase of the mastery I make to draw new talents from my soul. About to make a ravenous descent to fetch my masterpiece from beneath the rock!*

Fact of the matter was that he and Ramona, during the period of Urchin's absence, had thoroughly debated the relative merits of John Ward and Hirst and the casting process that he might employ to bring his idea to life. He felt that she could be trusted with his artistic vision and the direction he would take to achieve it. He wanted to invoke a vivid range of movement and axis, at once natural with an implied momentum. She was of the opinion that the idea, while evocative, might be challenging to bring forth in one of his little experience in casting bronze. Her challenge was telling as she interrogated him carefully on the process he had used to cast M3. The preliminary failures cast a cloud of doubt on his personal experience to accomplish this new casting himself; this combination of past failure and exploratory design nibbled at his wit. The debate—actually more of a dialectic between professionals—had accomplished two things; it exposed a faith in one another's integrity to demonstrably show the connection between folk art and classical art, and it forged an additional level of rapport between the two that aroused respect for both the thinking and understanding of bringing art closer to daily human interactions. Afri thought, If I can get Urchin gassed up about his own abilities and even stretch him in this project, he will experience a level of bliss rare in the souls of most African-American youngsters. *The country is impaled in programming, by the possibilities of the Internet, when most black kids—especially the boys—read so poorly.* Needless to say, Afri was determined for success, both in teaching and as an artist.

During his break, Afri Walker toyed with the folktale with which he was now so familiar. He quick-scanned the tale in a fashion some would call speed reading, which he had learned while taking a course with inimitable professor in Atlanta named Bud Foote. As a young collegian in that city, he had known that he would never be able to ingest all these experiences from long distance that had spurred the West to its great artistic accomplishments. But through reading he could grasp ghosts of its philosophies, chase the dynamics of its great ideas, possess knowledge of its trials and tribulations. He had learned the intellectual and emotional terrain of its artists. Practical technique was his immediate goal; thereafter, he would embark on a journey of its circular individual intellectual elocutions. He came up with the following iteration of the folktale:

In this version a master's apprentice is on a hunt and runs across a firebird's feather. The apprentice's horse warns the apprentice not to touch it, as bad things will happen. The apprentice ignores the advice and takes it to bring back to the master so he will be praised and rewarded. When the master is presented with the feather he demands the entire firebird or the death of the apprentice. The apprentice weeps back to his horse who instructs him to put corn on the fields in order to capture the firebird. The firebird comes down to eat allowing the apprentice to capture the bird. When the master is presented with the firebird he demands the apprentice fetch the Princess

Masterie so the master may marry her, otherwise the apprentice will be killed. The apprentice goes to Masterie's lands and drugs her with a wine to bring her back to the master. The master was pleased and rewarded the apprentice, however when Masterie awoke and realized she was not home she began to weep. If she was to be married she wanted her wedding masterpiece, which was under a rock in the middle of the Blue Sea. Once again the apprentice wept to his horse and fulfilled his duty to his master and brought back the masterpiece. Masterie was stubborn and refused to marry the master even with her masterpiece until the apprentice was dipped in boiling water. The apprentice begged to see his horse before he was boiled and the horse put a spell on the apprentice to protect him from the water. The apprentice came out more handsome than anyone had ever seen. The master saw this and jumped in as well but was instead boiled alive. The apprentice was chosen to be master and married Masterie and they lived happily.

Afri laughed at this iteration; ain't ready to jump in no water just yet! he said out loud, *musta been thinking bout that pine box in my damn subconscious.* He tossed it into the waste basket. But the thought of Urchin's gang—Las Siestas—troubled him. He knew that vast difference, one of being able to see difference in a commitment and zest for learning cultivated by an apprenticeship and the legal recriminations for learning, established and blurred by the approbations of slavery, were critical to his understanding. He promised himself to ask Urchin that question: what, in your mind, is the difference between an apprentice and a slave? Right behind that basket in which he'd tossed his ramified translation, on the pine box stood a new gaggle of featherbells brought to the studio by Ramona. *I woulda sworn that those flowery bells tinkled when I made that basket.*

Thought chased his mind to the skeleton of the bird once again; *the skull needs to be halved also, one side showing bone, the other completely natural to the naked eye. Remember, one wing arches high, the other waves low across the ground.* He glanced at his watch; *pizza and coffee for breakfast—not good— dust all over the floor, you'd think it was a blizzard in July.* Old M3 BONGED loud and clear just then, as Urchin rubbernecked his way through the door's entrance and froze with a stare. I know, I look like a snowman in July, said Afri. Nope, said Urchin smiling, You look like a ghost from Fort Pickering lost in a midwinter blizzard. Did you work all night? Afri said, I didn't sleep a wink brother—too much to do; good to see you! Did you think about how to construct the core, once we get the outer mold made? And remind me to get your contact info; you still staying at your Granny's? Yeah, said Urchin, but its kinda spooky being alone in that house. I lock it up but sometimes I hear noises and don't rest so good. Well, Afri said thinking about the pine box, it's nice and dark in that old pine box, so you can always take a nap there if you want to test your bravery! They both got a chuckle out of that.

Wow, you did get a lot done, said Urchin, once he'd gotten over the appearance of Afri and took several spins around the perimeter of the sculptures, eye-balling them for his mental archives. I like those —didn't know you were doing two! Oh yeah! Me and Ramona talked about both concepts and I wanted to see which medium would be easier for me. UPS brought materials for the ceramic molds a couple of days ago; FEDEX brought some stuff for the inner core—supposed to have a high refractory element. You think the furnace will be able to hold all that heat without a chimney? I know you want the bronze to stay hot longer so as to pick up details of the feathers. Well, we'll see Urchin, yes indeed, we'll see, said Afri. The boys that rebuilt it said it would stand up with that design I drew; indirect, curled venting is supposed to work, so we'll see. Whassup with you— you at peace with the Siestas?—I noticed your mural is significantly different from the masterpiece you first drew? The question drew an extra beat of hesitation. *Still stupid as ever,* slashed like a racing thoroughbred round the back of Urchin's mind, sizzling behind his eyeballs. He said, They be alright. Slipping into street jargon, thought Afri, *something's up, leave it lay for the moment.* Afri said, Well, I made two cinnamon buns, take one—you want coffee or cocoa, my breakfast was a pizza slice. Yuk, said Urchin, Cocoa sounds real good. Gotcha! said Afri.

Urchin got busy on the floor; he covered the same ground several times for thoroughness, polishing the passes up with a little sawdust on the floor, like he'd seen the janitor at school do. Remember Urchin, if you need anything let me know. Don't wanna get in your business, just letting you know. Martin and Malcom are before your time, but just so you know, they were both killed—assassinated for their efforts to liberate colored folk from chains of racial oppression—that kind of oppression can come from black and white folk, not just one or the other. So don't let you or your mind be controlled by anyone other than yourself. Okay, came back to Afri sounding half-hearted, but the brushing sounds of the broom had stopped—*so he was listening*, thought Afri smiling to himself. He laid the bun and cocoa out in front of Urchin on his return from the kitchen space. Look, I know you want to get to work on your personal masterpieces, but take this reading along–it's got a clear discussion about bronze casting—some call it lost wax casting—I want you to read it over the next few days—especially the part about sprues. And by the way, you've had several calls for orders, from both the gallery and some businesses downtown. Congratulations!

Urchin went about his chores, glanced at the materials Afri had chosen for him, and sat down to carve on his puppets. He could see that his effort was paying off—they were starting to really take shape. You know that guy—John Ward—when he started out with Kirke Brown, he was a paying student, then an apprentice before he moved on to his own studio.

But he was tough enough to know that he wasn't a slave—not about something that brought him joy and a few dollars—you're going to have your own place one day. Later that day, Urchin received several calls, one from a woman and another from a man; both asked him for prices on the feather quills that he made. Oh, forty dollars said Urchin; behind the necks of the Firebirds, Afri smiled, delighted at the young apprentice's business acumen; go lil brother, he thought. Well, I'll have to check that with my master...you can always mail it. I see, I see, yes I can have three ready for you...yes, cash and carry, sir...that's the deal. I will call you back to confirm the date and time—yes sir. Goodbye! Urchin reflected on the call somewhat miffed by the man's headlong manner. The fellow seemed brusque and a bit oily to the youngster and provoked a suspicion that he did not quite understand.

XVII

The painted turban that stood on the wall next to the train station appeared to be the work of Zorro; he was the best graffiti artist in Las Siestas, next to me. Nobody else could draw a lick; Zorro sought revenge when pissed off and got mean when his dander was up. The sight of it backed up my emotions to questions around the night of the rat debacle. I hadn't seen Bay Brother since the funeral; Parrot, LeMarcus and Zorro hadn't shown up. Bay Brother and I talked about what had happened afterwards and I learned that LeMarcus had left the car in the park and the three of them, along with the cousins, had run back to the 'hood without waiting to watch the cops and firemen deal with the mess. The police had impounded the car and LeMarcus' dad was super-pissed about having to pay a bunch of fees to get it out. Them polices charged both LeMarcus and Zorro wid reckless 'dangerment, said Bay Brother, once they found out thems the one who done it! They be real mad wid your ass lil brother, you runnin' off lak you done! Zorro got his leg burned real bad. Zorro say you ain't nuttin but a slave—a slave for another nigger. I tried to explain 'bout what you said, 'bout apprenticeships and all, but he jus' laughed, said that ain't noting but a big word for slave.

I was too focused on my carving and drawing to worry about the whole casting process straight-on; but the graffiti was a reminder that Zorro or LeMarcus, maybe both, lurked about. I organized my day to complete my chores straightaway, practice drawing (which copied the routine of my master), develop and create new puppets, construct my quills, and read up on the bronze casting process. For me, it was difficult to imagine how the casting would be executed; I had learned from my master to observe a procedure unfold, see how errors are corrected and repaired, contemplate revisions in the finished product. I was glad that I would only be responsible for a small but important portion of bronzing this bird. My master was beside himself with energy and effort. His blithe spirit had scoured the Memphis stratosphere in search of a fiery muse. Jealousy's hunt for talent and creativity had captured its prey, now entombed in plaster and clay. Fergus could relate to that—like his conductor, wishing to play or keep a steady beat, or a king praying for marksmanship, or rats desperate for wings to escape burn barrels.

My musings on sprues had been apportioned for me in advance and I tackled the means of losing wax and pouring bronze as best I could. A sprue, according to my reading, is a vessel through which molten bronze is introduced to a mold. Sprues are part of a gating system and serve as canals which allow the bronze to infiltrate the mold and attach to a negative, outer mold. In order to acquaint myself with the process and imprint the process clearly in my mind, I researched and sketched several drawings of a system of gated sprues. I could see how the sprues constrained the flow of liquid metal, formed a drainage system for the metal, and allowed the escape of hot gases and wax. Pictures of large buckets holding molten metal reminded me of the blazing reds and oranges of the firebird and the reddened seahorse. I never spoke of the call I'd received requesting three quills and information on progress of the commission. Granny was always of the opinion that I should tell some and keep some, when questioned about personal matters. I felt compelled to use that advice. However, I did bring up the time of the meet saying, Master Afri, I have a customer that wants to meet me at Marmalades for lunch tomorrow. I wanted to check to see if you will need me then? Afri said, A customer—that's terrific—I think I did hear you speaking to a customer the other day; of course you can go, and good luck with that.

And then for some reason, I started drawing feathers with my quills—practicing the construction of feathers, the vane, the quill, the rachis. I did this with both hands while learning the parts previously unknown to me by name. Even as I listened to the music of Stravinsky, this time played by the New York Philharmonic, I thought of an occasion when Bay Brother, frustrated by his inability to improve his concentration, started to shake in reaction to teasing by Zorro, who asked, What in the world makes you so dumb Bay? You don' need to worry 'bout readin' that stuff, shoot, ain't none of us gon' get jobs anyway. The school had no teacher that specialized in solving reading problems, there was no clinic or online way to address those issues on the Internet; fact of the matter was, asking somebody their reading comprehension score or level of concentration in measurements was considered an insult. The response could be quite crude; You crazy, course I can read fool!

    I scanned the materials Afri gave me on bronze casting with one eye on the refurbished furnace that stood on the far side of the studio, happy that the bricked contraption, with its lowered floor, had been engineered by experts. They convinced him that the chimneyless design would vent smoke. The tall plume of orange I'd seen at the park convinced me that a similar explosion inside the studio could tear off the side wall. The vivid sight haunted my escape to the magnolia tree right in the belly of old Fort Pickering. Maps and descriptions of the fort documented a tall watchtower built by Sherman, a total of fifty-five artillery pieces, a railroad and an ordnance department, all on the fourth bluff. Additionally, it was outfitted with a hospital, soldier's quarters, a saw mill, and quarters for contraband and refugees. I wondered if the defensive parapet was now occupied by the Ornamental Metal Museum. The printed documents faded before my eyes as I fashioned a new quill, adding a medium nib, from one of the feathers on my desk. *Match my energy;* my master had leveled the challenge at me—*whew! Just watching him sweat makes me tired.*

    I'm headed out to make my sale. Do you want me to bring anything back from Marmalades? Nope, said Afri, Have a good time and watch the urge to negotiate on your price; don't let your coin turn to dust, don't compromise the value of your product! There was that word dust again, I thought as I heard

M3 BONG from outside the door, gazing at a sky darkened by stratocumulus clouds colored much darker than the turban painted on that concrete wall. Heading towards the restaurant, my feet were light, almost as if I were walking in the clouds, excited about my appointment to meet with an admirer of my quills. I had one of my puppets too, stuffed on top of papers in my shoulder bag; perhaps this person would be interested in the purchase of a puppet. I felt like an entrepreneur ready to be a force hidden in the clouds, manipulating puppets—manipulating events and somehow in charge of a market which would bring money and fame. People with money and fame have chauffeurs, body guards, personal trainers, large houses, long cars, servants, slaves. I walked as if I had no worldly care, as if anointed by the gods of good fortune. Before I knew it, I had turned the corner at G.E. Patterson Street, passed The Arcade restaurant and arrived at the doorway of Marmalades.

Good Afternoon, said the waitress, Having lunch with us today? Yes, I answered glad to make it before all those dark and dusty clouds let loose with rain. Just one? crooned the waitress. Well, I'm supposed to be meeting a gentleman here—a fellow who wants to buy, with whom I have a business deal. An elderly gentleman? He might be here already...just this way and we can check. I followed her to a table located in the middle of the spacious floor. You must be Urchin, said the distinguished looking, white-haired man nursing a cup of coffee. Such a great pleasure to meet you. He nodded thank-you to the waitress, And of course to be the proud owner of one of your quills! Thank you sir, I said, Happy to meet you too! Well order up, this is on me. Forgot to introduce myself, my name is Wesley Hargrove, have you heard that name before? The name drew a beat of silence from me and I flashed memory to connect it with something special. Wesley added, I write reviews in the Commercial Flyer for arts events. Oh yeah, I said, I've heard of you. *You be the one wrote that review of Master Afri that we blew beans at!* What are you having? The wings here are awesome, but so are the BLTs. This lunch is on me, just to show my appreciation for your talent, said Hargrove. I think my master knows your name too, I said, trying to keep from showing the least sign of surprise or contempt.

We enjoyed a measured quiet as Hargrove sniffed the air in search of clues in my reaction to the sound of his name. How did you come to serve as an apprentice for one so eminent as Mr. Walker? Eminent? I said, Not sure I know what that means; *his manner suggested the sniff of a bloodhound!* Oh, no matter, said Hargrove with a chuckle, it means famous or outstanding. The waitress delivered our order saying, Wings and salad for you sir and for you young man, salad and a barbecue sandwich. For his part, Wesley Hargrove was completely elated by the presence of this Urchin, this apprentice of Afri Walker. Though intimately familiar with Rogets Thesaurus and thousands of adjectives to capture his joy, all he could think of was, *Goody.* I have been a big fan of your, uh, master—is that what you called him? Yessir. That's the way an apprentice addresses his superior in artistic endeavor. *The memorized words surprised me at their oiliness.* Hargrove nodded gracefully and said, I understand that you found him? Actually offered your services to him so as to learn about art? And so, is the work hard? I waited and cross-countered saying, I brought the quills you ordered, got three of them right here in my shoulder bag, further bending the conversation saying, This sandwich is really great. Oh yes, said Hargrove, lost in reflexive attention to the politics of apprenticeship, subtle silences and unfinished sentences designed to elicit information. Obviously you enjoy your work there! Hargrove added, I have your check all ready. Thrilled I said, Oh and I have one of the puppets that I made, thought you might be interested...when I become owner of my own business, I plan to focus on puppets. Aha, said Hargrove, mumbling past a chicken bone, that brings me to an interesting point, um, do you consider yourself well paid? I wondered about those two strings that travel through a dollar sign; *master of puppets.*

Hargrove continued, At one time I myself was an apprentice and though my apprenticeship led me in a direction different than yours, I am known for my eagle-eyed appraisal of talent. Urchin responded, Me, well paid? You are paid, are you not? said Hargove nonchalantly. Urchin studied the man's face for clues of meaning and said, My master treats me like an apprentice, a *student*-apprentice. Hargrove responded, Um I see—so let me assume that you could use additional funds, sums of money. The waitress came, took the empty plates, and left the check. Think about it, said Hargrove after she left, adding, And here is a check, said Hargrove placing the check on the table, You'll find it generous. Oh, I almost forgot, he added, I heard—by way of the grapevine of course—that Mr. Walker plans to prepare his new commission, The Firebird, right there in his Main Street studio, sculpt it, do the molds and casting right there himself. Pardon me, you said something about a puppet; please do let me see it. Urchin reached past jumbled papers and pulled the puppet out of his bag, demonstrating its movement and colorful structure. A masterpiece! cried Hargrove, All this talent on Main Street. Bravo, young man, splendid! Here, I'll take the puppet too, he said, pushing the three-hundred dollar check to Urchin. The Master's Apprentice! He shouted, brandishing the Russian inspired mannequin to nearby customers, Splendid indeed! I have not seen the piece personally, the sketches and all mind you. As Hargrove spoke, Urchin remembered he had one preliminary sketch in his bag; he squirmed and silenced his bouncing leg. Urchin folded the check, put it in his billfold, and said, Thank you very much for lunch; *which was not really about me, not actually about my puppets and quills*, It's a great pleasure to make your acquaintance; *Granny would have appreciated me using her phrase*. I like to compete in the marketplace, but you gave me too much money. Thank *you* Mr. Urchin, crooned Hargrove, The pleasure is indeed all mine; and I see you have included your card just like a rising entrepreneur. Your master has taught you well, especially in the arena of competition and artistic mastery. Consider it—the check, a down-payment on insight! Oh how I would love to see the sculpture as it stands, and surely you will help with the sprues and casting. You are aware of that word *sprues?*

Hargrove noted that Urchin missed that question, as the youth had reached the door, absorbed in the influx of customers bearing rain-splattered umbrellas and water-soaked clothing. It's raining, Urchin blurted, And raining really hard; The urge to escape the questioning clutches of this Hargrove overtook him and he said once again, Many thanks for lunch, and bolted out the door using his shoulder bag for an umbrella.

Urchin took long strides, hoping unsuccessfully to conquer cold raindrops with speed, and reached The Arcade quickly. An arm reached out, yanking him into its revolving door. On the inside of the restaurant, LeMarcus stood with his back to the exit-way. Zorro stood, wedged next to him inside the revolving quarter of glass doors. With breath hot and rancid he said, Hey stupid moth—ker, we been missin' you and your family been missin' you. You think you be some big-time apprentice sucker, but you ain't nuttin but another slave...and a jive, half-assed one at that! Done abandoned the hood, hangin' out wid–you be good at followin' orders—do dis, do dat, havin' lunch wid aristocracy...and shit! Yeah, done shit-canned yo boys. Betta watch out; you know what we do wid rats; rats dat don' respect their homies! The restaurant owner had grabbed a shotgun, now pointed at LeMarcus. Zorro saw this and bolted out the door, I found myself spinning in the circular doorway as they both zoomed up the street. I felt as though I was both slave and king, a big check in my pocket, but a big problem ahead. Bag in hand, I sloshed my way southward to the studio.

XVIII

Although I have a limited view of Memphis geography, I have seen drainage ditches in numerous parts of the city; I have also heard them called canals or channels. They are familiar sights next to Getwell Street and off Kimball Avenue. Since Memphis is on a series of bluffs, flooding is only an occasional experience. Nonetheless, it has been known to happen when rain is heavy; I have personally witnessed flooding, caused by leaves and trash on the street; which block storm drains or pool in low-lying areas. It was just this type of low-lying blockage that Zorro and LeMarcus had raced towards the train station on G.E. Patterson Street. Zorro was nowhere near as fleet afoot as LeMarcus, plus his gait showed a heavy limp (probably from the burns he experienced at the park). Even though my stomach churned and my heart stuck in my throat, I found myself chuckling as I watched LeMarcus slip to the sidewalk several times, first on his side and then full-faced on his chest, from his inability to get any traction at all! Zorro limped along in broad lunging steps and they both took irregular over-the-shoulder glances, wondering when a blast would explode from that shotgun. Their frightened flight truly tickled me almost as much as a silent Laurel and Hardy flick.

My clothes fared no better; to say I was soaked would have been an understatement. I watched them run for a few seconds and then continued my sloshy trot to the studio. Instinct infected my feet, terror made them move, and anger drenched me as fully as the heavy, incessant rain. My heart pounded. Hey! Came a voice, distant but familiar. I wiped wetness from my eyes, not knowing if it was tears or rain. Hey! You need a ride? It was Hargrove calling from his SUV, Jump in, I'm going your way! I'd had enough of him for one day, but was thankful that I could escape the rain if only for a few blocks. Bedump, bedump, bedump! his windshield wipers were going full tilt. I almost dived into the passenger seat. Wow! I said, wiping my face and forehead, it's really coming down hard. It was sunny and clear just a few days ago, now we have this—and it's kinda cold too, I said shivering.

Couldn't help but notice those toughs trying to rough you up, you know them? said Hargrove. Kinda, I said, they been tracking me for a while. Bedump, bedump, blotted out my voice and he said, well you better be careful. Look, he continued, Sprues are the channels, the canals that carry hot bronze in and out of the molds. If the sculpture, I mean the *sprues* get screwed up—*accidentally* of course—you might be the one to get a show at the gallery with your puppets and quills, *you* would be the one called master! Just an observation; think about it. Tell me when to stop, I can hardly see in all this rain. He leaned over the steering wheel, using the back of his hand to free the inner windshield of condensation. *Jeez! Is he offering me a bribe? Does he want me to play the part of Judas?* I was unsure of his words, yet felt warmed by the idea that I could be a master so soon, and me having never set foot in a gallery before this summer! The preliminary sketch of Afri's Firebird design, at rest in my shoulder bag, made the back of my brain itch. Here! I said. Hargrove stopped the car just as we reached the studio entrance. Before I knew it, I had drawn the sketch—one of several Afri had given me—from my wet shoulder bag and handed it to Hargrove; *scratched that itch*. Thank you Urchin, he said surveying the damp, crumpled mass greedily, This has been a most satisfying luncheon. Please do stay in touch; you need not give my regards to your master!

Before crossing the street, I stepped back, took a look at the turban graffiti painted on concrete, and vomited. The rain fell in torrents now and rivulets of streaming water ran alongside the curb. I stepped into the street and was almost hit by a car, wiping my mouth with my palm. The sound—Bedump, bedump, bedump, of the wiper blades still rang in my ears.

***

As Hargrove drove back to his office, he maintained a steady pace. The Bedump, bedump of his windshield wiper blades reminded him of an old metronome; the rain had slowed considerably since its original downpour and he hummed out loud strains of the Hallelujah chorus, joyful in the seeding of his plan to sabotage the construction of the Firebird sculpture. And it wasn't that hard, he thought to himself. *Damn wench encouraging niggers to attend concerts; mongrelizing the great accomplishments of western civilization*. Suspicious by nature, he would relish the crash-and-burn of Ramona's plan to pull together the idea of folk and classical music being both expressions of the human spirit, relish the control and power he wielded as one who donated money to the gallery in largess, and cherish the thought that his minimal talent as an artist still allowed him to guide the direction and growth of the gallery, both with the power of his pen as critic and the jangle of pennies in his pocket. *The princess was stubborn and refused to marry the critic even with her dress until the artist was dipped in boiling water;* the image of planking Ramona had crossed his mind more than once, but he dismissed the thought peremptorily. *To hell with all that Firebird bullshit, once a king, always a king—king of the hill—the sun never sets on the king! Haaaallelujah! When that sucker is on his knees, I'll have that MemNoire too.*

* * *

Ramona sat in her office reading an unsolicited draft of a report delivered to her by the ethics committee of the Board of Directors. Never before had the committee submitted such a report to her regarding actions taken with regard to the Director's Choice Award, or any other award for that matter. It was a committee chaired by Wesley Hargrove and she read it slowly, highlighting the portions of it that she found ominous or distressing. The report outlined in copious detail elements of the Fitzgerald Act that related to apprenticeships. She had been surprised at the receipt of this document, surprised that Hargrove as one of independent wealth and means, would take such an interest in an anonymous youth hired by Afri out of the goodness of the sculptor's heart. The portion of the Act that caused her grave concern was the following;

Registered Apprenticeship program sponsors identify the minimum qualifications to apply into their apprenticeship program. The eligible starting age can be no less than 16 years of age; however, individuals must usually be 18 to be an apprentice in hazardous occupations. Program sponsors may also identify additional minimum qualifications and credentials to apply, e.g., education, ability to physically perform the essential functions of the occupation, and proof of age. Based on the selection method utilized by the sponsor, additional qualification standards, such as fair aptitude tests and interviews, school grades, and previous work experience may be identified.

She immediately placed a call to Afri Walker. Afri, I have a document in front of me that could potentially create a problem for your commission. How is your time tomorrow? I see, what do you need me to do? Said Afri, adding, and Hello. I'm sorry, greetings! Said Ramona, Look, I don't want to discuss this on the phone, but save an hour or so tomorrow after lunch, say one or two. I'll come by early to sit for Urchin. I think he's almost finished with my puppet. We can't discuss this in front of him! I'll come by, sit for him, and then find some way to excuse either him or ourselves. Hargrove is up to a trick I think to derail your commission. I wish I could come by tonight, but I already have several engagements lined up. Okay, said Afri, You sound concerned. I am, said Ramona, but I need some time to figure out how we can side step this problem. In the meantime, you need to carefully think about exactly what tasks you have set up for Urchin to perform in the casting process for the Firebird. Gotta go, and don't forget! After hanging up, Ramona took a deep breath to calm herself. She combed the folktale for answers; *If she was to be director she wanted her masterpiece, which was inside plaster and clay in the middle of the Blues. The archer mounted his seahorse, cast the sculpture, and fetched the masterpiece.* Marriage hadn't crossed her mind; the jumble of her thoughts annoyed her. She reread the draft and placed it aside thinking, I never wanted to be a princess and I certainly couldn't imagine being attracted to hectoring Hargrove or a king—now Afri—?

***

Fergus was at home practicing the clarinet part of Stravinsky's Firebird Suite, which he had arranged. For him, the words brought the music to mind and he practiced the parts diligently, with an electric metronome, transposing the part, alternating the speeds, adjusting his reed for the ultimate in fluency, articulation, and creaminess of sound. The music, the spirit of each enchanted character was part and parcel of his soul. In the Memphis Philharmonic he had played it for a variety of conductors some of whom in the recent past looked like constipated mannequins, bedeviled stovepipes, praying mantises, and humpbacked beetles. Now he was greatly favored to additionally enjoy the solos of oboes, flutes, and bassoons, since he gave many of those solos to himself. The sound of the instrument had enchanted him since boyhood days—even those cold winter days when he'd seen old men standing in wait for odd jobs—*warming their hands,* Fergus thought, *over burn barrels swearing, shooting craps, drinking whiskey, feinting each other with bobs and jabs.* He stopped to play some long-tones. Magic stepped to him, whacked the image of a burn barrel past a long, black telescope, and stretched it into a telescopic 22-caliber rifle with him in its cross-hairs. The animated image played as a film reel once during just such a solo, leaving ruddy, ruby-red tears on his black patent-leather shoes. He nursed, then tickled himself with these thoughts: *the clarinetist begged to see his horse before he was boiled and the horse put a spell on the clarinetist to protect him from the water. The clarinetist came out more handsome than anyone had ever seen. The conductor saw this and jumped in as well but was instead boiled alive. The clarinetist was chosen conductor and married the symphony and they lived happily.* Tomorrow, his trio would serenade Afri in his studio to celebrate the commission of the Firebird sculpture and show Urchin some horsehair.

***

Afri Walker took pains to make a robust pot of coffee meant to last deep into the night. Time became organized in a target. He stayed the course on his plan to do one of the castings himself. He was determined to see the process through himself and the revisions to the furnace had cost him much of his savings. Fergus had called right before he took Ramona's call. Occasionally, he reflected on the negotiation through which he and Ramona had arrived at compromise on the final two sculptures. Instead of the Bitches Brew he'd often heard about in developing singular visions in this type of situation, they'd drawn up qualities both felt would make the finished product unique, mysterious and yet enchanting. Yes, but Hargrove's psychology is messianic, said Ramona. He has little use for indigenous folkart, or Mozart for that matter. His ideas and heavy-handedness make some board members quake! she'd said. Members of my board have tried their hand at being artists and failed miserably. I get the feeling that some of them are jealous! Unfortunately, just as in sports, artistic matters should be relegated to the artists! Stravinsky had quite effectively managed his business legacy. In Stravinsky's Firebird Suite, King Kastchei's egg—housed in his castle—signifies his immortality. The prince destroys the egg, thus liberating the princess in the ballet. The prince kills the king with a sword provided by the Firebird. That destroys the king's quest for immortality. Afri thought about this as he reviewed the process, which he outlined carefully; make silicone/ceramic mold, make wax positive, attach sprues and gates, invest core and pins, divest wax-pour bronze, chase metal, add patina. He eliminated all other documents from the walls. Even with the coffee, the usually energetic sculptor found himself sluggish, dead tired on his feet. *Maybe a walk around the block, some fresh air; maybe that will do the trick.* He mounted the stairs to change clothes, eye-balled the bed, took off his shoes—oh-boy—lay down and conked out on the spot.

Urchin stumbled into the studio, headed straight to the restroom and retched once again. He rinsed his face and used toilet tissue to clean his pants, shirt front, and tennis shoes. The scent of the pine box teased him towards it; stepping closer to it, he found himself soothed by the smell of the wood and its peaceful, sedate wooden interior. Urchin lay himself down inside the pine box, closed his eyes, pulled down its top and slumbered before hitting its bottom. When Ramona entered the Main Street studio, The BONG of M3 was not heard by her or anyone else. She'd arranged to change her meeting time to later in the week. Where the heck is everybody? She wondered. Her perusal of a ropeless M3 fell upon a list of casting steps Afri had taped to the wall. She was concerned about the production steps Afri planned for Urchin to perform. This question haunted her: What did Afri need to do to effect the boy's registration as necessitated by the Fitzgerald Act?

XIX

Ramona stood in the middle of the studio for a few moments, aware that Afri had not been expecting her. *Maybe he's upstairs or gone out for a moment; maybe something bad has happened. Gee, I just talked to him earlier.* She noticed no BONG from a rope-less M3, no challenge from the unlocked door. Darkness came late in July and the place possessed an eerie quiet as she started to feel more than a bit uncomfortable. She called him by name, quietly first, and then knocked gently on the door; *no answer!* Remembering the cell phone in her pocket, she dialed his number. The phone rang several times and went to automatic answer. Almost immediately, her phone rang as she went to the door to look outside. Hello, she said. Hi, said Afri sounding a bit drugged and hoarse, Thought you had a meeting? I got it changed and–and, well I'm downstairs, said Ramona, I came right in and there's no one here! Gosh, Urchin must have gone home, said Afri, Give me a minute, I fell asleep. I left the front door open so he could get in. Too many late nights working I guess. I'll be right down.

She studied the studio carefully. The featherbells that she had brought drooped badly and she threw them in the trash, making a mental note to bring fresh ones on her next visit. Then she sat on the pine box to take a long, hard look at the single model left of the Firebird. The clay sculpture had a fierce majesty to it, one which captured the ideas and technical juxtapositions they had discussed; *the piece is indeed powerful.* Ramona allowed her imagination to envision the patina it would hold, once recreated in bronze and glowing in the space of the gallery. In a sense, this was her masterpiece as well as his; the final step in a process to bring to the new wing, an initial work to honor folk art and classical art, the traditional and the contemporary, and hopefully encourage artistic hopefuls that their works could seek placements in the gallery. It was a gamble that she thought might cost her dearly if the piece failed as an attraction for potential patrons. Then she let her mind ramble back to the draft recently received from Hargrove; *The eligible starting age can be no less than 16 years of age.* She wasn't sure and it could be just a technicality. Urchin might be 16 or seventeen even, and it could be that he was just taking lessons. *But* what if he were hurt, or scalded—*dipped in boiling water*—came to her mind and she shook off the thought. Just the insurance would probably eat up whatever gain Afri would receive from the commission—and then there would be the adverse publicity, she thought.

Hey, great to see you, said Afri looking refreshed and wearing his familiar smile. Glad you could make it after all. Say, you're all wet and you look worried. Did you get something to eat? Oh I'm good, she said sounding too proud to admit hunger.

Well I've got some leftover ribs in that mini fridge; going to heat them up...let me take your coat and turn up the heat a bit; been a kinda downcast day and – you're shivering! Ramona released the buckle on her trench-coat and freed the straps; Afri felt her hands press into the flesh of his forearms, squeeze the muscles with her fingertips. Look, she said, You have worked so hard on the piece, with all these political ins and outs—you have been very patient to deal with all the bullshit it's taken to get this thing off the ground. Just sit with me for a minute; do you have a bottle of wine or something? I think that would be enough for me right now, just to calm my nerves. Jeez Ramona your hair is soaking wet, said Afri, you look like you're really worried about something; did I do something that created a problem? Ramona put her arms around Afri's neck, and buried her head in his chest; *this feels better than what I was worried about.* He'd heard no sobs and guessed that she might be catching cold or just having a difficult day; when he drew back she would not release her purchase; instinct told him that she must feel the hardness that grew between them, and felt embarrassed. I'll get the wine and light a candle; grab a towel for you to dry your hair. Neither of them had acknowledged the attraction generated over time, through communicating and negotiating the politics and vision of the artwork of their mutual visions. Here you go, towel and a glass of red wine. Afri Walker dried her hair for her as Ramona took small, long sips of Mulderbush Rose.

Urchin floated in la-la land many thousands of miles away. The urgency of his violent retching was calmed by the smell of knotted pine, the dark interior of Afri's memento of mortality, and the cotton clouds of the turban fluffiness seemed to haul both his body and soul to that place where choirs sang one of Granny's favorite songs: *Swing Low Sweet Chariot*. To the casual, it would appear that he rested as if a babe and needed only a blanket of some sort to sleep through the night. The serious observer would recognize the signs of food poisoning, a mild sweat, an ever so slight discoloration of the facial skin, and of course a lingering effluvium of vomit slightly disguised by the fragrance of the cranberry scented candle lit in the studio. By any standard of measure, he would surely be awake, had it not been for the ping-pong sized aberration, the knotty hole, located at the north end of the knotted pine box; he rested, breathing deeply as if a somnambulist.

In his dream, he heard a *debump, debump* sound, lighter and more gentle than the one caused by Hargrove's windshield wipers. It was more like the gentle rock of Granny's chair, lisping back and forth in gentle movement, watching him with gentle eyes from her favorite place. Debump, debump, and gently singing *Swing Low*. He saw her gnarled fingers, her knobby knees, heard her scratchy yet oddly velvet voice, singing those words and they comforted him. Strangely enough, the pine box seemed to float on waves of the Mississippi, when that river sloshed against the granite bricks that held it with its banks...*debump, debump*. Every so often, he heard her sigh, a long languid serene breath, sigh and pant—bleat—as if she were a lamb or sheep, headed to the promised land in her dream state. He knew that heaven was up there some place. A place where the Golden Rule held sway in clouds of cotton that would be there for him someday. And he saw her smile, riding on the back of a reddish orange seahorse floating over a Mississippi sunset. Glory be! was what she had said, and that was what he believed...*debump, debump,* Oh yes, oh—mmm yes, and he heard that too...*debump, de, debump, bump*, and the change of pulse and pattern didn't bother him, no not one little bit. They had called him that when he was jus' a tiny baby—Little Bit—and the sound soothed him, caressed him, made him feel alright, even if he was in a coffin. *Debump, bump, bump.* In a coffin? He moved, trying to change position finding that it was done with more effort than was usual for him. Though the sound seemed far away, it lurked around him, through him, as if he were one with—debump, de, de, de, bump, bump—it. Now the voice seemed less scratchy and more harmonious in its bleats, and he thought of a violin or cello. That's it, like the one I saw in the picture, like the one Fergus is bringing that has horse hair. But its not a horse; its more gentle than a horse and slower, *debump, debump—and the voice saying , So sweeeeet!* And more bleats, *that's not so, it's Oh, oh, oooooh! Debump.* This change of rhythm disturbed him, roused him awake? I am an instrument of music; the rapture of rhythm and harmony vibrate—*debump*—through my body! And then suddenly it stopped—*DE-BUMP!*

Sensing heaviness above him, Urchin managed just enough movement to put his eye to the small hole; *I can get through this hole,* and he squeezed to no avail, settling for a posture in which he could peep to the outside. The cranberry fragrance came more fully to his nose and the small, dancing blaze of a bright candle cast a fluttering glow animating the shadows and sculpture of the Firebird; *vivid.* This silent movie flickered like a film. *That's the second hand on the gallery's grandfather clock*—no the swinging braid of a...woman! *with no clothes, and her braided hair swings across her back*—like the second hand of a grandfather clock—as she—no, it's, it's—Ramona? The radiance and glow of her body made her appear as if a princess mounting the Firebird, *and the firebird would morph, become a Seahorse, to take her to the bottom of the Deep Blue Sea to fetch her Master's Peace! Surely this is a dream!* Closeted in his pined labyrinth, gentle waves rocked his confusion to join a peace which dissolved beyond candlelit muskiness; Urchin's thoughts floundered to deep sleep.

***

Are you watching this crap, asked LeMarcus, worried that his buddies wouldn't get to make a plan to rein in the behavior of one of its prime recruits. I like John Wayne, said Zorro, He's got a cool strut man, almost as bad as Denzel and he knows how to shoot. Did you see that shot he just made? Bad dude! They lounged in the basement of Zorro's house, drinking beer and smoking joints; Zorro's mom wouldn't be home til late and Zorro's cousins, Bay Brother, and Parrot had joined them. H-h-his gun ain't so hot, said Parrot I s-s-seen automatics that could wear his honky ass out f-f-f-four or five times 'fore he could get o-o-off a-s-shot! The ancient black and white screen fluttered and rolled every once in a while as if it had caught the Memphis syndrome; all acts are interpreted and defined in terms of black and white. Man I can't stand to watch that fake crap, said LeMarcus who walked over and turned off the set, And I got this damn dog hair all over my clothes! Don't y'all ever clean this place up? he added, brushing off his jeans. Clean t-th-th-this place up? echoed Parrot brushing off his clothes as an afterthought. Hey man, we're just getting to the good part and this ain't *your* crib! blurted Zorro. We got to figure out what to do about Urchin, said LeMarcus, Got to bring that brother down a peg or two! Ain't nuttin, said Bay Brother, he jus tryin' to get goin' in the world, tryin' to compete, make something outta hisself; you jealous? Kinda stupid if you ask me, going 'round' collectin' feathers, and shit, said Zorro eyeballin' the silent set and walkin' over to turn it back on. Anybody want another hit? he asked. Tonto sat in the corner, yawning, licking his paws, and sniffing the strange smells for signs of adventure. Trying to m-m-make some of h-hisself, said Parrot. Well he be breaking all our rules, ignoring get-togethers, going 'round incognito, actin' lak we don' even exist! Needs some teachin' if you ask me. What we gon' teach 'im man? thought you didn't want nothing to do wid teachin', seeing as how you hate teachers and all, said one of the cousins.

Wayne had just broken a beer bottle over the head of a poker player and Zorro said, Maybe that's what we need to do, break a beer bottle over his head, teach him some respect; he be dissin' us pretty regular. Why he be collecting feathers for? said LeMarcus. Making pens—calls 'em quills—least that what he said at the funeral, said Bay Brother. See, here's that program from when his massa won that thing called a mission. Sells them quills here and there! Here and t-th-th-there, said Parrot. Bay Brother offered Parrot another swig of beer which he waved off. I need a pair of gloves like Wayne be wearin'; makes it easier to knock somebody out! said Zorro. You don' need to be worryin' bout that, said LeMarcus, Light in the ass as you are, you couldn't knock out a feather! Who you be homes, Mike Tyson or somebody? I'll make you a deal, said Wayne, holding one of the bad guys by the collar. LeMarcus reached for the television set once more and Zorro stepped to him, grabbed his hand hard snatching it away. Tonto growled, understanding the friction between LeMarcus and Zorro and asserting his kingship in the domain of the basement. LeMarcus fish-eyed the German shepherd, eyeballed Zorro, and relaxed in the chair. One of the cousins was deep into rollin' another joint, fired it up and took a deep inhale.

Well I ain't selling shit but hard times, but when I make me some money, first thing I gots to do is get me a Palomino; ain't gon' be ridin' no nag. Gon' get me a Palomino mustang! Said Zorro. On TV Zorro rode a white stallion, said Bay Brother getting a little bored with the conversation. Whatever! said Zorro, turning the television up a wee bit. LeMarcus shook his head, Dats all Wayne ever rode wuz nags! Man you got a conversation problem or sumthin'? said Zorro, All you ever want to talk about is Urchin; he be jus' one dude! You jus' like all them old dudes, drinkin' and talkin' 'bout when they wuz athletes, who they wuz jammin', what they wuz drinkin'! This be the twenty-first century dude; be some other things to talk about—other than old times. Buck jes' wanna be happenin' after he gets fifty under his belt, Bay brother said, Urchin be chasin' ideas and shit, not jus' women, booze, cars and hemp! The movie cast a dim flicker across the room, strobing waifs of clouds and jangling furtive eyes. Tonto whined and changed position. Well if y'all gon' jack him up, you best decide you gon'—LeMarcus jumped out of his seat and grabbed the second cousin by his shirt collar, Gon what! Little mother, gon' what? Tonto's ears had long been perked and he sent a warning growl across the room. LeMarcus clearly had his dander up and seemed intent on making a display of leadership prowess to the second cousin; the first cousin flashed a knife. Wayne had slinked across a dirt street and fired several shots at a runaway bandito. Tonto had risen to a standing posture, as Zorro yelled, What the hell are you doing man? Get your hands off my cousin, and he grabbed LeMarcus by the arm. Simultaneously, Tonto leaped across the room, flying as if making a dunk-shot, and bit into the backseat of LeMarcus' britches. Parrot sat goggle-eyed, though his beer bottle was unfortunately on the flight path; it sent a cool spray all over his crouch. Off my c-c-c-ousin he said, O-o-off! Bay Brother rose and made for the door; the suddenness of the dog's flight drew both fear and laughter from him at once; *Ain't about to tackle no big-assed mutt!* LeMarcus made it out just as Tonto made for his throat. Since darkness had yet to fall, bystanders along their homebound route took long gawks and ganders, pointing and laughing at his exposed backside, his bare buttocks, his naked discomfort. Since Bay Brother was taller, well chiseled, and much heavier than he, LeMarcus made no effort to chastise him or try to control his hefty chuckles. Bay Brother was the only one of Urchin's cohorts who had read the folktale. He might have summed the situation up this way:

The Firebird and Ego. In this version a gang's Zorro is on a hunt and runs across a firebird's feather. Zorro's horse warns the Zorro not to touch it, as bad things will happen. Zorro ignores the advice and takes it to bring back to the gang so he will be praised and rewarded. When the gang is presented with the feather they demand the entire firebird or the death of the Zorro. Zorro weeps back to his horse who instructs him to put corn on the fields in order to capture the firebird. The firebird comes down to eat allowing Zorro to capture the bird. When the gang is presented with the firebird they demand Zorro fetch Ego so the gang may lead her, otherwise the Zorro will be killed. Zorro goes to Ego's lands and drugs her with a wine to bring her back to the gang. The gang was pleased and rewarded Zorro, however when Ego awoke and realized she was not home she began to weep. If she was to be married she wanted her wedding dress, which was under a rock in the middle of the Blue Sea. Once again Zorro wept to his horse and fulfilled his duty to his gang and brought back the dress. Ego was stubborn and refused to join the gang even with her dress until the Zorro was dipped in boiling water. Zorro begged to see his horse before he was boiled and the horse put a spell on the Zorro to protect him from the water. Zorro came out more handsome than anyone had ever seen. The gang saw this and jumped in as well but were instead boiled alive. Zorro was chosen to be gang leader and married Ego and they lived–happily?

XX

As a student-apprentice—or at least that was the term we used—for Master Walker, I was in preparation to become a self-supporting artist. Did that mean I was a flunky? Did I owe allegiance to Afri?? Should I have given Wesley Hargrove my sketch of the Firebird design? Would Las Siestas continue to turn up in odd places with schemes to harass me into their gang? I had witnessed some of their techniques secondhand, now up close and personal. Usually a neophyte was instructed to rob a store, steal a car, kick some poor unfortunate's butt, install graffiti somewhere to infect body and soul. Each escalation acted like a screw in the wall to become gradually intrusive psychologically and physically.

The business at Riverside Park showed me what could happen; yesterday's episode brought me even closer to physical harm. Do as we dictate or you'll be next! That was the message. I had overheard Ramona and Afri discuss the politics of his commission, talk about the resistance of board members to non-classical artworks. It seemed to me that works in the gallery were creations of a European diaspora. Was Afri their puppet—a stringed puppet—dancing at their behest? Is that the point of cultural society? To create puppets? He had recognized some ability in me, hired me to be his helper and given me an introduction to his way of creating art. He had refused to sell a painting and now this person wanted to know about, learn about, possibly sabotage his effort in creating his latest vision—prevent it from becoming a reality. And I had betrayed a confidence, his confidence, by sharing a sketch. I wasn't a real happy camper and Granny wasn't around to talk to: shit! I turned this over in my mind before deciding to sneak out early for breakfast. I climbed out of the pine box, put on my shoes, and fish-eyed the candle on the table right across from the hole in the pine box. From that pine box I really could see the candle! On close inspection of the trash can, I realized that my so-called dream was in fact reality. The beautiful woman I had seen, or thought I had seen, had indeed been Ramona. Afri had stolen my princess! In no time flat, my sense of betrayal reversed course; he deserved my betrayal, deserved to be sabotaged, deserved to be held accountable for this theft, deserved to be *my* apprentice!

      I dampened M3 so that it wouldn't BONG as I left. I walked past familiar sights: trash cans, shop windows, nude mannequins sporting hats, billboards hawking tickets...Grizzlies tickets, patrons heading to the Amtrak station. Every face became that of Ramona; Ramona in a basketball jersey, Ramona nude under a hat, Ramona's braid swinging in the breeze in long strides to catch a train! When I saw Ramona smoking a Virginia Slim's cigarette. I spoke to myself; Urchin, get something to eat right away! And it was true, I did need to eat, my body felt weak, and the love of my short life was gone. I was heartbroken. As I returned to the studio, I even saw

Ramona's face under that damn turban Zorro had painted!

Urchin, we're going to need that ladle over there to be in position to pour molten bronze into the mold I'm making of this sculpture. The thing had been cut up into pieces! *Here he was, King Walker, giving me orders—again!* When we get going, he said, you're going to think you are looking right into the scarlet red eye of the Firebird with a ringside seat! We'll have on those masks over there and those gloves. Gonna sweat like monkeys in the Congo lil brother! *Don't hand me that lil brother shit!* The furnace had a shiny refractory barrel (*that's what King Walker called it*) over the sand pit in the floor. We are going to have a pour party! I heard *poor* party and thought; *ain't poor no more big brother! The King continued speaking to his puppet.* When the moment comes, we'll line up all your puppets so they can see the action. Now a ladle is a container used to transport molten metal; it's a barrel like receptacle lined with refractory material for molten bronze some call a crucible. These ingots and bricks will be heated at 2,500 degrees and poured into a shell, three-sixteenths thick, gated and sprued by you my man. Yeah, 2,500 degrees Urchin; that is some kinda hot—ruby red hot!

King Rooster spoke again, Urchin we are close to the defining moment, the moment of magic when we point the efforts of the past few months to the minute in which we make our vision a reality.

Oooohh-weeee! All those bones, organs, feathers, and beaks. You can record this story with some of your quills lil brother; *will you puuulllease, stop calling me that! I am your Judas! I* pinched myself to quiet my inner voice. I said, I've got those bones memorized...k-k-m-Master Afri; the cervical vertebrae, the clavicle, sternum...the keel. Bravo, my master said; *I could not say king out loud.* I'm going to use this silicon on the feathers...enhance the definition of muscles on this side, he said, triceps, serratus, biceps...and on the skull. Watching his enthusiasm and boyish joy, a flame of shame dusted over me. It seemed fanned by the leaf of paper given yesterday to Wesley Hargrove.

    Afri then showed me a drawing of the way in which he wanted the tools to be set up, much like a surgeon's tools—all ready to go at a moment's notice. This is yours and last, but not least, we have in this box, the sprues and gates we'll be using to control the flow of bronze into the cavity between the outer mold and the inner core. Your part will be tricky, my friend—very tricky, but I am counting on you. Once I get the insides waxed and the outsides molded, I'm turning it over to you—I'll help you—to do your thing. Okay, so these tools—hammers, chisels, torches, and such, will be the ones I use to chase the bronze, once we get it fired and break it away from the ceramic outer mold and core. Then we'll have bronze duplicates of our sculpture which are *hollow* inside. Once we get to that point, we have to reassemble the whole thing and polish it. For the life of me, the hollow-matrix portion of the process left me somewhat baffled. Anyway, for the next few days we waxed the insides of those ceramic parts and I studied the sprueing process; we must have waxed and re-waxed wings, legs, the main body, neck and skull a thousand times! Every time I thought about molten lava I shivered; those poor rats never had a chance in those hot flames; I also took pains to learn about the shoes and headgear I would need to keep from becoming a flaming statue.

We're almost there Urchin, almost there! By the way, I have some information I need to get from you before we pour. It clarifies your role as student-apprentice and protects you in case anything goes wrong. Ramona assures me that this registration makes your employ here legitimate and I have documented your faithful and regular attendance. It also guarantees your salary of one-hundred and fifty dollars a week, with you working six hours each day. Take it with you and read it; I need to have it signed before we do the final pour. I hadn't seen Ramona for a while as she was involved with a fund-raising campaign, but on the last few days before the campaign started, she seemed quite pleased with her puppet (and bought a few quills to boot). I watched for clues on her rapport with Afri, but learned nothing to give the impression that they were indeed lovers. When I signed the contract, I smiled inwardly at the thought of receiving multiple checks; and me, a few months ago, plum broke! A hollow man can serve many masters and kings? I knew that eventually I had

Las Siestas to deal with plus Afri and Hargrove, but for now I was good. Money was my masterpiece at the bottom of the Blue Sea.

Just before the pour, I received a registered letter from the gallery; I signed for it! Looks like your quills are becoming popular, said Afri when the letter arrived. A serious entrepreneur! I opened the typed letter assuming that it was from the gallery gift shop. Although it was on gallery stationery, it was handwritten and signed, Hargrove. It read:

Here is an additional check for three-hundred dollars. Do not forget that sprues are the most important part in pouring the mold; CLOG the sprues!! I will contact you immediately thereafter with your bonus check. With admiration, Wesley Hargrove.

I continued to perform my duties, even upped the ante a bit by making my efforts efficient; even my reading became more efficient, as my master shared his personal tactics of reading for speed and comprehension with me. Needless to say, I read a great deal of information about sprues on the Internet. Sprues could be made of wax, metal, or plastic and there were many ways to accomplish the final casting. Obviously, we needed metal sprues for molten bronze. We would use refractory sprays on top of the metal sprues. I had the folktale memorized, was caught between puppeteers pulling my strings with violence and money, and had lost my first real crush; I was not inspiring to behold! At this point, my most prominent thought was to make confetti out of that damn folktale, which I did even before the big celebration! I was hell-bent on ruining that pour, putting a wrench into it, jack-up his delivery calendar, to render my master inept! My view of the firebird folktale follows;

> In this version an artist's apprentice is on a hunt and runs across a firebird's feather. The apprentice's horse warns the apprentice not to touch it, as bad things will happen. The apprentice ignores the advice and takes it to bring back to the artist so he will be praised and rewarded. When the artist is presented with the feather he demands the entire firebird or the death of the apprentice. The apprentice weeps back to his horse who instructs him to put confetti on the fields in order to capture the firebird. The firebird comes down to eat allowing the apprentice to capture the bird. When the artist is presented with the firebird he demands the apprentice fetch the Princess Vassilisa so the artist may marry her, otherwise the apprentice will be killed. The apprentice goes to the princess's lands and drugs her with a wine to bring her back to the artist. The artist was pleased and rewarded the apprentice, however when the princess awoke and realized she was not home she began to weep. If she was to be married she wanted her wedding dress, which was under a rock in the middle of the Blue Sea. Once again the apprentice wept to his horse and fulfilled his duty to his artist and brought back the dress. The princess was stubborn and refused to marry the artist even with her dress until the apprentice was dipped in boiling water. The apprentice begged to see his horse before he was boiled and the horse put a spell on the apprentice to protect him from the water. The apprentice came out more handsome

than anyone had ever seen. The artist saw this and jumped in as well but was instead boiled alive. The apprentice was chosen to be artist and married the princess and they lived happily.

XXI

When Ramona left Afri's arms late in the night of their mercurial tryst, Afri grabbed his flashlight to walk her to her car. He quickly placed the flashlight's beam on the turban across the street saying, Urchin's buddies are thumpin' his poor little brain with reminders of their influence; they are reminding him of what happens to partners leaving the gang. Yes, I noticed that—Can only imagine what the face beneath that turban looks like! She said. Call me when you get home so I know that you arrived safely, said Afri. They shared a goodnight kiss and he watched as she pulled into the dark, desolate street. She knew she had a problem and ran scenarios through her mind on the way home. After some thought and texting him on her safe arrival, she went to bed and slept soundly. In the morning she called Marsha, her secretary at the Brinks Gallery. Then she called Afri. Hey, she said. There's that lovely voice again, said Afri. Hargrove felt dissed when you wouldn't sell him that painting. I know, said Afri, Money can't buy everything. MemNoire serves a purpose that he wouldn't understand! That underscores the rationale for his poor review, said Ramona. F—k his bad review; I'm over that! Good, then I need you to be at the gallery at one o'clock today and I need you to trust me, said Ramona, I've got to deal with some politics. Folks don't always pick up on politics in the arts, he responded. I know, but where there are people, there are politics—especially in the arts! No problem—I'll be sure to act nonchalant and wear a tie, said Afri, Be a respectable black artiste. Unnecessary, she said, Just be yourself—and thanks for a very lovely evening. The pleasure was all mine; promise me that we will repeat it in the near future? Promise, she said.

Marsha, I have a emergency and need to meet with as many board members as possible some damage control. Okay, said Marsha, What do I need to do? Alright, here's what I need. I want you to send an email out to all the board members. Tell them I have an emergency situation—one of our board members, Wesley Hargrove—sent an email around containing a preliminary sketch of Afri's Firebird sculpture! I think that he's trying to sabotage its construction. The email also lays groundwork to embarrass Mr. Walker's use of a youngster as his apprentice; lay the framework for a legal challenge of a kid he is trying to help. Now here's the thing: I want to schedule the meet for one o'clock. Send the request via both email and text! Most of them will not be able to make it, but I want to leave the invitation open for everybody. They should understand that I need to exercise make an immediate decision and lean hard on the task force chairs to be there! I don't think Hargrove sent this to anyone outside the board. One o'clock! Okay, said Marsha, got it! And see if any of the CEOs of arts organizations are available; invite the president of the MPO, the zoo, The Hooks Library, Opera Memphis—see if any of them can make it; I need the best minds in the city around for this one. One more thing, said Ramona, Order lunch —a large Caesar salad, some spaghetti and meatballs, lots of cut-up fruit, coffee! And, be sure that Afri and Hargrove will be there! Absolutely must—be sure you get positive confirmation from them! Okay, said Marsha. Thanks Marsha, you're a gem. I'll be there in less than an hour. And some apples Marsha, some apples and digital music; Mozart string quartets.

Ramona called the emergency meeting to order at 1:15. Marsha had followed through nicely: everything had been prepared on time and the scents of fruit, spaghetti, meatballs, apples and coffee blossomed in the Gallery conference room. The seven members who made it gossiped mildly, with Afri and Hargrove some distance from one another. Missy Shepherd, the one black member, sat front seat center to be sure—I ain't missin' a thang! Folks thanks for being here on such short notice; I promise not to keep you for more than an hour, said Ramona. One of our most distinguished board members has sent a crude picture to the entire board without my sanction. For me this is most distressing, but before taking any action I want to get your opinions on what my reaction should be. Let me remind you that I respect the professionalism of each one of you; we are, have been, and continue to be a fabulous team. My experience in Memphis leads me to believe that we are having a strong and positive impact. If our citizens, particularly our black citizens, cannot expect open arms from cultural organizations—the libraries, museums, educational institutions, schools, zoo, ballet, symphony, churches—then we are fooling ourselves in the grand experiment designed to develop a lasting participatory democracy. The awesome lack of support for public schools by institutions of higher education in this city may make the Memphis bluffs quake; but that is not our immediate problem. Before I continue, I want to get your reaction to a leak of what I consider my prerogative as Director, I want to hear feedback from you, positive, negative, and neutral. So, I'll give you five minutes to discuss, and then go around the room giving each of you two minutes. Fact of the matter is I could be overreacting to this leak, since it has yet to be public. Feel free to get in groups if you want. And think of positive ways to put your ideas in place, now uh, Marsha will be our timekeeper and we will not vote. I just need to take the temperature in the room.

Some of the members gathered around Afri, others remained neutral, two bankers moved over to chat with Hargrove. Administrators from Opera Memphis, and the Memphis Philharmonic arrived late, curious about the request with intent to support Ramona, though they were not aware of the immediate issue. Ramona continued, That could mean allowing the aesthetic of blackness appear in concert halls, in galleries, in museums—in short in contemporary masterworks—not only in the abstract and refracted by Anglo artists, but in the concrete as represented by artists of the African diaspora. So, you've got five minutes. What started as a hum whirled to a buzz; by the end of five minutes she received many verbal comments. I think this breach of protocol is embarrassing to the gallery but not catastrophic, said a library administrator, it runs counter to the process usually considered as teamwork, and he added, One big thing we have identified as missing in our institution is a feedback mechanism for patrons. To many, we are seen as elitist and know-it-alls. I love the idea of a FolkArt Wing and applaud your effort. This seems to me to be a negative commentary on the choice you made and an attack on your decision, said another member. Another group leader said, This leak to our minds, seems to be addressed to both you and Afri—we think you are correct in seeking advice and hope you will take steps to correct the situation. Our group thinks you should not tolerate making semi-public a decision which might result in an embarrassing legal question, though the person should have talked with you prior to sharing this sketch with the board members. Other board members thought the email to be gauche, reckless, or immature. Most agreed that the choice to unveil the design of the Director's Choice Award was hers and hers alone. Some hot debate took place between the members and Ramona thanked the crowd for the advice they had given her; she immediately turned to Afri and Hargrove saying, Afri, Hargrove, I need to see you both for a few minutes in my office. Marsha, would you join us for a few minutes?

Gentlemen I think you have met previously. You both know I am concerned with this leak. Probably the best thing we could do is hash out the background of this issue, or since you both are adults, I could leave and have Marsha transcribe the dialogue that takes place, so that whatever issue remains is solved. Or, you could choose to do a dialogue journal–equal time, equal space—between the two of you that resolves this situation. I have no problem doing a dialogue journal with Wesley, said Afri. Hargrove looked a bit baffled. A reckless dissonance tinkered behind his eyeballs. He wanted to press the point of Urchin possibly working in underage servitude at Afri's studio, wanted to exude his legendary bravado in speaking to points of classical symmetry, consonant harmony, elements of balance and perspective, techniques of an elaborate baroque and romantic eloquence. Instead he found his tongue to failing him, his bombast fading and said, I think I'd better pass on that one, as Marsha took notes, I don't consider that the best way for me to express my opinion. You mean, you don't consider yourself an artist or a man's equal, said Afri. What a helluva impertinent thing to say! bellowed Hargrove. Well I'm both of those, so belly up to the bar lil brother! Said Afri. Asshole, barked a red-faced Hargrove as he made for the door.

***

I continued my employ at the Main Street studio, learning to peer through metal masks, protective clothing and boots. I could feel the excitement jangle in my knees, though I could also feel that there were things, important things, that I did not know. My plan to sabotage the sprues remained secreted in my breast. I labored mightily to repress my jealously of the master I was hired to serve and betray. Eventually the plan I settled upon was that of infusing those channels which fell under my jurisdiction with minute particles of clay, so as to slow, backup, and misdirect the flow of bronze into the mold, thus clogging the process and rendering an ugly, misshapen mass of mess as a finished piece of sculpture unworthy of display. I could feel a different kind of tension in the studio and had a sense that Afri knew more than he was willing to share with me. Even so, I attached sprues, sprayed them with ceramic materials, and then added additional layers of ceramic and refractory materials to visibly ensure a smooth pour. Master Afri was pleased when bricks and ingots of bronze arrived; I was pleased that I had signed my contracts and looked for those singular moments when I could meet the obligations of my master in the main, and the obligations of my sinister benefactor on the sly. I had a bit of a respite from Las Siestas; I wondered where they had gone and continued to take circuitous routes to Granny's. Every now and then some of her church members would bring by a plate, but in the main I was anxious and kept out a sharp eye.

Fergus came by to wish us good luck on the pour. M3 BONGED as he walked through the door and he said, You know, we should record that bong, amplify, and set it up to play all day, every Sunday city-wide in memory of Martin! Man, my trio broke up; the cellist left town cause she just can't afford to play on the salary they're paying her—says she can't afford to go into more debt. I found this violin bow in the pawn shop—hope it didn't belong to anyone in the Memphis Phil—anyway, guess what kind of hair is on the bow, Urchin? Horsehair? I answered as if a question. Boy, you are on the ball. Afri, what you been feedin' this boy; he gets smarter every day! I couldn't bring the trio, but I did bring a view of our concert where we did the Firebird. And—I wrote down the exact places where I want to show you my conducting technique, and how I would conduct those parts! And you can see how much better I am than some of these awful clowns we got that perch on our podium. Well Ramona just gave a great update on team play, he said without getting into particulars that Urchin would overhear. Yeah, talked about groups being a team—she was downright inspiring!

Team? Shit bro, you kidding me? Conductors and musicians ain't no team. Probably ain't a conductor in the country that would negotiate his salary alongside the musicians. That's a team. They won't tell us, but we haven't had a conductor lately that would bear the same percentage cut of salary that they ask of the musicians. Ain't no team 'bout that shit! We got board members that think musicians and athletes are slaves for conductors or coaches; say man, tons of athletes get paid more than coaches—that never happens in an orchestra. Course, none of this comes out in investigative reporting, mainly because the investigation part is—missing—DOA, my man. Fergus took the violin bow, and said, This is my baton and this my good brother Urchin is how the pattern of four/four time should look. Something like an upside down T; simple right?—Wrrroong! Here's what I get in the orchestra. He put his arm in a position of extreme contorted-ness, bounced up and down with great anxiety, and ricocheted on downbeats like Zorro had pounced next to that burn barrel (right after one of those rats leaped his way and set his foot on fire). Profound iracundus! And I sit there watching that shit and wonderin', okay which part of your arm is the beat? Elbow, finger, wrist? Upper shoulder or your nose! If I could take that damn clarinet out of my mouth, I would ask that question. You know what the conductor would probably say, Hell dude—your guess is as good as mine. It takes a conductor, especially one of the ones we've had lately, to truly F-up a beat.

Winded, he sat down for a minute, then said, You would think—given the issues that our orchestra is having, that they would use audience building as a linchpin—that's what De Frank did—especially now that the Internet is around; how about excerpts and mini-lessons online, pdfs of scores, ask for reviews from patrons, definitely hold on to gospel concerts, maybe a fanfare competition for the great unwashed (with the composer talking about composition), put that conductors talk online. A baton lesson on-line—just so folks know the difference between three/four and four/four—Oh, and a Batman's skylight so the concerts get announced, mobiles of orchestra members in the hallway, dress up the hall with some chandeliers! Man, I could go on and on. Believe me, the musicians are working their collective asses off! The parent of one of our guys said, And now the sunofabitch wants to be a conductor! You can always tell when an organization is shuckin' and jivin'; they never want to here back from the public—from the patrons; it's just a big dig me, take this you heathens! The Anglo part of the West is still entrenched with its so-called stranglehold on the classics. And not a feedback form in the house! If asked about conductors, my advice would be to seek this soul amongst a trinity of plasticity and a lyrical child of opera, an ensemble master born of rhythmic acuity, and wise patience, learned from a love of people. The handmaiden of this triumvirate in simplicity resides! Pardon my rant, but just one more thing; critics should talk about what they learned in a concert and encourage folks to get out, help their kids be literate, and attend all that wonderful music, maybe even young composer's challenge competition to write some pieces, if only for movies or cartoons!

Man, old Fergus was fired up!

XXII

I stayed away from the studio for a few days, laying low to avoid Las Siestas. And that mold with all that ceramic crap was fired up too, once Afri got that furnace rolling and the ladle hot! My street credits with Las Siestas had nose-dived into negative territory. So I hung out around Fort Pickering with the hobos. I was sure that Las Siestas stalked my trail, but managed to escape them for those few days. I remember drawing some sketches of my brain, caught as it was between old man Hargrove and Zorro, and air brushing one on the old marine hospital out of pure frustration. For some reason, my mind wandered to that second sculpture and I wondered what had happened to it. My fret was short-lived and my old magnolia tree brought me tons of comfort; I found her shade soothing.

Afri still slept when I got to the studio early on Saturday. On my last visit to the studio I had tested the sprue and gating system for the final pour with water, and found two or three critical spots that wouldn't show up to suggest that anything was wrong. We had chased wax out of the targeted cavity and had things all ready to go. Afri put the furnace through its paces and was waiting for some additional bricks of bronze to arrive. Old M3 BONG-ed on my entry and I immediately got to work by preparing my shoes, mask, and gloves. While he got up and took his shower, I inserted little portions of clay in those critical spots, making sure that they were unnoticeable to the eye. When Afri stepped from the stairs I was practicing my conducting technique with that violin bow Fergus left.

    Hey lil bro; figured you were still hiding out from your homies, said Afri. Those bronze bricks got here yesterday and we are all set to go! Glad to see you made it. Ramona may not make it; there's some sort of parade going on—did you see all those sawhorses in the street?—So I'll talk to her about it later! Bought some sausage biscuits yesterday, he said, For breakfast, you want one? That sounds real good, I said and put on my protective gear. While the ladle was heating up, Afri cranked up some music; instead of *The Firebird Suite,* the player sang Put On, by local rapper DrummaBoy. Once we ate and downed coffee, Afri donned his gear and we got started; that ladle had the red hot, mean looking eye of a drunk crocodile. It looked meaner than anything I'd ever seen, like hot lava foaming in a volcano.

    Once that ladle had stoked and brewed those bricks, we shifted the prongs on which it was connected to the funnel which captured the red lava and poured that stuff into the lips of the funnel, watching raptly as it spewed and bubbled its way into the cavity of the sculpture. I held my breath, hoping that the thing wouldn't gag and vomit; I couldn't imagine the kind of upset stomach I would have if it were me; God! Outside, I could hear men shouting and giving orders; must be getting ready for the parade. That was the one day that I had matched the movement, the sweat, and the anxiety that haloed my master; the one day when my *energy* had matched his! My blood tingled as I watched the bronze soak into the funnel and I was even more pleased when some flowed out of the overflow gate. Afri stepped over to old M3 and struck the bell which gave its approval with a huge GONG!!

It would be several days before the result would be known. We had to chip away all the sprues and gates and strip away the ceramic that encased the cavity of the sculpture. Afri shot Ramona a call saying, Everything went well and we had a good pour; seemed like the hot metal went much better than the pours I had for M3. I recall my thoughts:

In this version a master's apprentice is on a hunt and runs across a firebird's feather. The apprentice's horse warns the apprentice not to touch it, as bad things will happen. The apprentice ignores the advice and takes it to bring back to the master so he will be praised and rewarded. When the master is presented with the feather he demands the entire firebird or the death of the apprentice. The apprentice weeps back to his horse who instructs him to put corn on the fields in order to capture the firebird. The firebird comes down to eat allowing the apprentice to capture the bird. When the master is presented with the firebird he demands the apprentice fetch the Princess Masterie so the master may marry her, otherwise the apprentice will be killed. The apprentice goes to Masterie's lands and drugs her with a wine to bring her back to the master. The master was pleased and rewarded the apprentice, however when Masterie awoke and realized she was not home she began to weep. If she was to be married she wanted her wedding masterpiece, which was under a rock in the middle of the Blue Sea. Once again the apprentice wept to his horse and fulfilled his duty to his master and brought back the masterpiece. Masterie was stubborn and refused to marry the master even with her masterpiece until the apprentice was dipped in boiling water. The apprentice begged to see his horse before he was boiled and the horse put a spell on the apprentice to protect him from the water. The apprentice came out more handsome than anyone had ever seen. The master saw this and jumped in as well but was instead boiled alive. The apprentice was chosen to be master and married Masterie and they lived happily.

Smiling, I poured another cup of coffee for myself and one for Master Afri and went outside to relax and get some fresh air. The parade was in full swing by now and bands from two or three high schools joined in the merriment. The street was lined with onlookers, many of whom had come to the area to make purchases at the outdoor market for produce. To tell the truth, I was ashamed of my effort to trip up the mastery of my master and seemed frozen in my thinking . Somehow, I had been convinced that my apprenticeship was an act of servitude, of slavery. From that moment to this very day, I am stunned by my acceptance of the theories of Las Siestas, of not only chucking my chances toward mastery, but also threatening the chances of Afri Walker who had given me the opportunity to thrive, to compete, to learn, and to survive in an environment which would become ever more competitive and challenging. I was in this mental posture as I watched the parade, watched the majorettes and instrumentalists march down the street, with their stunts and swaggers.

I think the girls get prettier and prettier, said Afri, watching the batons of twirlers fly high into the air, Beautiful legs, he added. Ranks of clarinets, trumpets, flutes, and sousaphones barked and whistled as they went by; a full complement of trombones played strands of *Seventy-six Trombones,* while the next band strutted down the street drumming out the melodies of Stevie Wonder's, *My Cherie Amour!* The tune brought my mind to Ramona, her lithe figure disappearing into the candle on the night of my greatest loss. Before my eyes there stood a mighty looking Arabian, the tail of this horse waving in the breeze almost to the beat of the music. It was as if Fergus was astride the beautiful animal conducting the *Firebird Suite* right in front of me; Afri pulled me to the side, Never stand right behind a horse, he said, You could get the living shit kicked out of you! Flies tried to mount the immaculately disciplined stallion's broad backside; the hair of its tail, instead of drawing melodies from violin strings, swatted those pesky insects.

As I stood there among a throng of Memphians, Afri went back inside to make sure all was well with the studio; I better check that furnace, make sure nothing is blazing away, he said. Transfixed as I was in the cheerful crowd, I barely noticed the movement of a sparkling white turban, bouncing past the clowns and majorettes prancing down the street, to the tune of James Brown's, *Papa's Got a Brand New Bag!* Beauty Queens on floats waved and smiled their way down

Main Street. A tall clown with bulbous painted lips and huge shoes waved at me and yelled furiously in my direction; Get out, get out of the street! I flashed on the mural across the street and stepped into a vanishing void to cross over and examine it closely. I knew that Las Siestas lurked with intent on imposing their will, but the bright sunlight, the throng, the wonderful blue sky arrested my fear. I put my finger to the graffiti; scratching it for tangible clues about its maker. Zorro, I said to myself in a whisper, recognizing the brand of paint. You damn right sucker and your ass is mine! I looked squarely into the malicious eyes of Zorro, then bolted down the street like lightning hoping to lose him at the station's corner and dissolve into the crowd. He caught me and jumped my back; I squirmed and threw him to the ground using a spin-move mastered on the basketball court, then landed a solid kick to the place of his leg burns. Zorro screamed a mighty howl and retreated, leaving me a split moment to make a mad, fervid dash to the front of Afri's studio. At that very moment a huge cheer arose from the crowd with excited members crying, Oh look up in the air, way up next to the sun! Airborne before all eyes arose a huge balloon in the shape of a red bird. I was later to learn that this ballooned red bird was a gift to Afri from Ramona, signaling the casting of the second sculpture at a professional foundry in Eads, Tennessee.

The sky-bound mass floated like a Goodyear blimp and was led by a bevy of grounded runners intent on keeping it tethered and well behaved. It was obviously commercially made—designed to imitate

Afri's sculpture—and sought to bound about in swirls and dives, hovering over the mass of onlookers and showering the crowd with grains of popcorn! The mounted policeman on this majestic, dappled Arabian witnessed our *mêlée,* had seen Zorro chase me on the train station side of the street, seen me scuffle in horror; he and his mount stood trapped by the column of parade just under the railroad tracks. With some difficulty, he trotted the horse to and fro on the station side scanning for our whereabouts. The Amtrak railroad tracks now stood above his head, twelve feet above street level. To my utter horror, LeMarcus appeared just above the mounted policeman, stood above his head, brandishing his father's half-mooned Yemeni Jambiya, immediately above the rider. From his position, LeMarcus leapt down on the horse in back of the shocked cop, slicing him at the neck, severing his head and sitting cocksure in his saddle! The brazen act froze many in the crowd, and angered others. Rocks, apples, oranges and curses pelted LeMarcus. Other unfortunate souls braved death to battle him with reckless abandon, holding whatever appurtenances they could find. Hordes of shocked witnesses scattered haphazardly; other frozen witnesses shrieked in panic and sent gasps catapulting through the air. Oh my god, cried one man, slipping and skating in pools of blood; others cried, Help, help! and made mad dashes through alleys, side-streets, and handy corridors. Bedlam overwhelmed the crowd as a panicked Afri frantically dialed 911 on his cell phone.

He's after *me* Master, I yelled pushing Afri towards the studio door, Get in the studio, go inside! Zorro had possession of my leg again, cocked his fist and gave it a punch, narrowly missing my jewels and landing in my groin. I kicked him in the chin, yelled, Get off me dammit! and hammered him across the back with my elbow. In his attempt to guide the stallion to where I stood, a turbaned LeMarcus—still mounted on the Arabian horse—trained his sights on me, casting a swoosh of the sword inches from my head and striking a string of the Firebird balloon, causing it to sway and buckle above the fray. I heard loud screams of, Get him! and Sonofabitch! jamming the airwaves. A crashing nose dive of the unanchored colossus, the huge Firebird replica, caused the horse to unleash a frightful roar and rear straight up in the air; LeMarcus was thrown to the ground and a volley of gunshots rendered him a bubbling quiver on the ground, his pooling blood running in rivulets towards the severed skull of the policeman. Several nearby women fainted on the spot as screaming sirens closed in on the hellish scene. Afri pulled me up from the street saying, Get the hell inside!

XXIII

To this day, I lament my lack of focus and energy during the course of my tenure as student of artistry. I had been mentally bovine, suffered from lack of physical endurance and possessed by bouts of greed. Worst of all, I sought to control the mastery of my mentor. In my deluded inability to understand apprenticeship, I sabotaged my own quest for mastery. Hindsight helps in defining maturity, but opportunity can be stingy and baffles the young with multiple guises. Nowadays, I make my living fashioning puppets; I also mount puppet shows at the Orpheum Theater for giggling groups of school children. Occasionally, I fashion a quill or two; I scribe this tale with one of those instruments! Often I think of that old pine box, Afri's reminder of his mortality. He understood that young boys of color—girls too—face serious obstacles in their quest to become, not just proud Americans, but citizens of the world fluent in many languages, conversant with artistic masterworks of all flavors, perceptive and yet understanding of many worldviews, and effective in their hold on the American Dream. For them, Martin and Malcom are twin goalposts; if their dreams falter unrealized, then the American Dream waxes corrupt: *period!* As I would later learn, Ramona and Afri had a backup plan for casting that second sculpture; as director of the Brinks Gallery, she had professional contacts all over the Memphis area. The pour at an Eads foundry had produced a spectacular sculpture, putting an international halo in the crown of Afri Walker.

A quick synopsis of Las Siestas may help clarify the sum of their purposes. The members of Las Siestas suffered various fates. LeMarcus died from his wounds at the parade; his mom cried mightily at his funeral, Oh he was such a good boy! and the officer who wounded him almost lost his job. The person under the clown outfit shouting at me to get out of the street was Bay Brother. Bay is now a state representative in Nashville; when fall came his mom took me in when school started so that I would have support finishing my senior year and obtaining my high school diploma. His academics took off after he inhaled Bud Foote's Reading Tutor, housed on my computer! Zorro never finished high school; occasionally, I see his name in the paper for petty crimes, though I have yet to see that he is involved with drugs. From time to time I run across Parrot; usually, it's in the winter and he takes toothless swigs from a bottle of Old Irish Rose while keeping his hands warm over a burn barrel. He is the polar opposite of Hargrove; he always asks *me* for money, ha!

The Opera Society found me through Fergus. Afri terminated my apprenticeship once school started; he offered to talk with me at the end of the school year, once I had received my diploma, but I was well aware of my betrayal of his trust and sent a letter thanking him for the opportunity; I was man enough to do that. I made it a point to shred my sketches and drawings regularly, so as not to expose my creative visions or planned designs.

I was asleep for a long time though I thought I was awake. My work—abortive as it was—left me with a formulaic, if not thorough understanding of the work of an artist. My experience with an aspiring, struggling artist—working to mine his craft, to realize his vision of an ancient folktale and show its connection to an orchestral masterwork, had taught me much, mainly about sweat and vision. It gave me the opportunity to witness a plan of action, a program of learning, and the structure of a path to realize artistic vision. Those are numerous who were jealous of Afri's commitment to his vision and the disguise of critic was just one of many guises. My mistake was one of immaturity and jealousy; but I vowed to never again have my thinking defined by another but rather to think globally, statistically, and artistically—provided that my decisions correspond to the Golden Rule. Through that lens, I can see how cultural institutions have failed black youth of the country, and continue to do so. But, those are not the only ones failing these youth.

Fergus continues to be a friend and from time to time invites me to an opera. From there, the opera folks have invited me to present short synopses of upcoming operas in schools as puppet shows. My shows familiarize students with the story behind the opera and mimic some of the arias and action in these stories. Fergus loves the zitzprobes—the sitting rehearsals—that put orchestra and singers together to probe and investigate the score of music. When you listen to a real masterwork—and all works written by classical musicians are *not* masterpieces—you start to understand the work that goes into creating pieces that sparkle through centuries of listening, looking, reading, or performing. Afri's Firebird might be in that category; time will tell. Once I realized that I would be making puppets for a living, I started taking classes in ballet. Stravinsky's Firebird was originally written for the ballet. Of course, I had no real talent or gift—at least that was my thinking in the beginning—but gradually over many years, I got better in my endurance and more agile in my ability to accomplish the various positions. As I became more familiar with French terms defining movement, I practiced the motions and positions with my puppets; I built my puppets in such a way that they could demonstrate the positions. The cabriole, a fast step in which extended legs are beaten in the air, remains an impossibility for me...though I try! My vision is to realize the ballet through puppetry. If you think sculpture is hard, try ballet and let me interview you afterwards. I have logged many days and nights in pursuit of perfecting the movements of my puppets to do ballet; this is a work in progress!

When I visit the schools, the students ask me how I learned to do this kind of work. The lethargic, cool and detached approach which engulfed me is not the one I recommend. In fact, I gradually dropped this approach, once I witnessed the energy of Afri in that Main Street studio. Granny gave me a really good hint about that when I helped her in the kitchen. Granny said, When I sit down, then everybody can sit down! Fergus said the same of Elsa, one of his teachers in Michigan; Man, she knows how to practice until the notes sweat from speeds, from analysis, from transpositions, and from memorizations! As I get closer to my artistic vision for my puppets, I make my movements efficient, sturdy, and reliable—just like I make my puppets. Nowadays, folks like to give us peeks into artistic beauty through the psychosis of criminality, the anti-hero. Fergus played portions of the *Quartet for the End of Time* for me by this fellow named Messiaen; he composed in a Nazi jail, though he was far from a criminal. But then Nazis and gangs define your values and decisions for you, in advance!

Be that as it may, I often take my puppets to prisons. Inmates are spellbound when I revisit the tale of the Firebird; I speak of the various characters, snake my way through a series of interpretations of the tale from various points of view; the archer, the princess, the critic or conductor, or king as the hero. In fact, I use the folktale as a prism. Gang members in jail almost always ask the question; But my leaders in church always seem to have crime or pimp-dom as a background, before they have an epiphany and are called to preaching. I love this question and fully embrace it; fact is, it gets my juices flowing. For me, criminality and usury point to a lack of leadership integrity, lack of Golden Rule empathy, and a desire to not only misunderstand the social environment, but to multiply the problem in church groups with flagrant violations of personal integrity. And untrained preachers to boot! How can you expect a psychotic, crime-laden mentality to enable the quest for the Golden Rule, labor for stout craftsmanship, enable a search for the artist in each of us. That's where the arts come in; learning an art supports personal discipline in developing craftsmanship, the elementary echelon of artistic endeavor. And this is exactly what I achieved at Master Walker's studio: craftsmanship! For giggles and kicks, I pieced together this slight parody to honor M3. One day I hoped to have one of my own!

The Firebird and Ego. In this version a Brotherhood's Ego is on a hunt and runs across a firebird's feather. The Ego's roots warns the Ego not to touch it, as bad things will happen. The Ego ignores the advice and takes it to bring back to the Brotherhood so he will be praised and rewarded. When the Brotherhood is presented with the feather they demand the entire firebird or the death of the Ego. The Ego weeps back to his roots who instruct him to put civil rights on the fields in order to capture thefirebird. The firebird comes down to have a voice in the struggle allowing the Ego to capture the bird. When the Brotherhood is presented with the firebird he demands the Ego fetch the princess Vassilisa by any means necessary so the Brotherhood may roost with her, otherwise the Ego will be killed. The Ego goes to the Princess's lands and drugs her with an Afro-American spiritual, Free at Last, to bring her back to the Brotherhood. The Brotherhood was pleased and rewarded the Ego, however when the Princess awoke and realized she was not home she began to weep. If she was to be roosted, she wanted her masterpieces of art, necessary for a revolution of values, which was under a rock in the middle of the Deep Blue Mississippi.

Once again the Ego wept to his roots and fulfilled his duty to his Brotherhood and brought back the masterpiece. The princess was stubborn and refused to confab with the Brotherhood even with her masterpiece until the Ego was dipped in boiling water. The Ego begged to see his roots before he was boiled and the roots put a spell on the Ego to protect him from the water. The Ego came out more handsome than anyone had ever seen. The Brotherhood saw this and jumped in as well but was instead boiled alive. The Ego was chosen to be Brotherhood, roosted with the princess and they lived
happily.

Next in my journey comes the mounting of the Seahorse; I certainly intend to seize my masterpiece at the bottom of the deep Blue Sea. Suffice it to say that my witness to Afri's ethic of workmanship towards his vision enabled me to duplicate that ethic in my own work, my own passionate endeavor. For that I am truly thankful!

Made in the USA
Lexington, KY
19 December 2017